BOOK TITLE

Daughters of the Holy Light

Noor & Noga

Inspired by real characters and actual events from the river to the sea - 2014

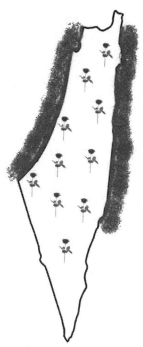

AUTHOR NAME

Nasser Najjar

BOOK TITLE

Copyright © 2021

All Rights Reserved

ISBN: 9798342897341

Dedication

For all those who left our world sharing their last words with me during the Israeli war on Gaza in 2014, believing that I was their last hope.

I'm sorry that I failed and couldn't do more for you and for your loved one to keep you among us. Know that there has not been a single night that has passed since then without hearing your voices, your screams and your fears.

Consider this book as an apology for not being able to do more. Rest in peace, and maybe I will someday too.

BOOK TITLE

CONTENTS

Dedication	4
About the Author	8
Prologue	10
Events Leading to the 2014 War	16
Chapter 1 (Ahmed)	20
Chapter 1-1 (Ahmed)	22
Chapter 1-2 (Ahmed)	30
Chapter 1-3 (Ahmed)	39
Chapter 1-4 (Ahmed)	44
Chapter 1-5 (Ahmed)	52
Chapter 2 (Noor)	55
Chapter 2-1 (Noor)	56
Chapter 2-2 (Noor)	67
Chapter 3 (Tony)	73
Chapter 3-1 (Tony)	75

Chapter 3-2 (Tony)	84
Chapter 3-3 (Tony)	92
Chapter 3-4 (Tony)	116
Chapter 4 (Ariel)	124
Chapter 4-1 (Ariel)	125
Chapter 4-2 (Ariel)	133
Chapter 5 (Mahmoud)	146
Chapter 5-1 (Mahmoud)	147
Chapter 6 (Sami)	161
Chapter 6-1 (Sami)	163
Chapter 6-2 (Sami)	171
Chapter 6-3 (Sami)	181
Chapter 6-4 (Sami)	189
Chapter 6-5 (Sami)	208
Chapter 6-6 (Sami)	225
Chapter 7 (Noga)	239
Chapter 7-1 (Noga)	241
Chapter 7-2 (Noga)	251

BOOK TITLE

Chapter 7-3 (Noga)   262

Chapter 7-4 (Noga)   276

Chapter 7-5 (Ariel's Recording)   281

Chapter 8 (Marwa)   293

Chapter 8-1 (Marwa)   295

Chapter 8-2 (Marwa)   316

Chapter 8-3 (Noor's Letter to Sami)   319

Chapter 8-4 (Marwa)   321

About the Author

Nasser Najjar was born as a Palestinian refugee. He lived his childhood in the United Arab Emirates; moving from the UAE to Gaza Palestine in his teenage years made him see the world differently, realizing that a lot must be done to make this world a better place. He finished his studies at the Islamic University of Gaza. Nasser worked in Journalism and human rights organizations; He was the former spokesperson and head of communications for the International Committee of Red Cross during the 2014 war on Gaza. He was also a researcher for Human Rights Watch and had documented violations committed against civilians in Gaza and refugees along the Turkish-Syrian border in 2015. In addition, Nasser had worked for a UN agency as a production manager. He also wrote for some papers such as USAToday, Al-Monitor, Gulfnews and worked as a producer for New York Times. Now Nasser moved to Vancouver Canada where he is accomplishing his degree in TV production.

BOOK TITLE

Page Blank Intentionally

AUTHOR NAME

Prologue

I kept on delaying publishing this book because at some point I started believing that the world failed the Palestinians. At some point I started believing that the world accepted the reality for Palestinians to remain occupied with no rights, delaying their lives and dreams of living in a country of their own with dignity from generation to generation. Yet in May 2021 I was impressed when I saw hundreds of thousands all around the world supporting Palestinians in Jerusalem, Gaza, the West Bank, and Arabs Israelis and chanting "Free, free Palestine". The world spoke and wants a free Palestine. This book is a gift for all those who believe in a free Palestine.

As it is hard to find two people who share an identical opinion regarding the Palestinian-Israeli conflict, I have no doubt this book will be controversial. The novel will discuss different groups of people who lived in the Holy Land. On that small piece of land, one group of people enjoys all their rights and privileges, whereas another group is denied every basic human right. This book will talk about the elephant in the room. It will talk about Palestinian rights, how they are denied the a right to live, the right to move, the right to establish their state, the right to fall in love, and most importantly, the right to feel safe.

I noticed through living among the main two ethnicities over there that Israelis see Palestinians only as a threat and Palestinians see Israelis only as occupiers and why there is no trust and peace.

The one and only truth that everyone agrees on is that this conflict has lasted for over seventy years and is still ongoing to this day without an expiration date. Unfortunately, there seems to be no solution on the horizon as long as the occupation does not end.

In my opinion, there are only two options as long as the current political status quo remained as it is—either a two-state solution on the borders of 1967 or one secular state for all. Other than that, the cycle of violence won't find an end. Of course any changes in the powers will come out with different results.

Archaeologist Eric H. Cline mentioned in his book "besieged Jerusalem" that the city was attacked 52 times, captured, and recaptured 44 times by different civilizations.

This sad reality shows how important this city is to everyone, This city was the destination of knights and saints as much it was for tyrants and sinners. It is wrong to say that Jerusalem belongs to one group of people. It belongs to all of us. It belongs to humanity.

This book will not focus on politics or history like thousands of other books. Over here, I will share with you what the daily life looks like for both of my people and the Israelis in both peace and war time—what they eat, how they sing and dance, what people do during conflicts, and how they easily commit to both love and war and switch between them as it's a walk in the park.

This book is all about people. It will discuss the hardships that people are going through over there, how the Palestinians' basic human rights in the West Bank and Jerusalem are violated every day, and how Palestinians over there get detained for no reason other than being the indigenous people of the land; how Gazans are living in continuous fear of the coming war against them; how Palestinians in Israel are considered second-class citizens. This book will also discuss how many Israelis have been torn apart between their harsh history and the guilt that their nation was built on the suffering of others.

The ideologies and thoughts of the characters in this book reflect the outcome of living in vastly different environments on a small piece of land, and their lives interact indirectly. And despite that, the characters' lives change each other; it makes sense in that they never met.

Each character will share life from their point of view in an entire chapter. Whether the character is a child with big ambitions, a rebellious woman, or a foreign aid worker trying to make the place better, a fighter defending what he believes is the right thing to do, or a devoted lover. Most probably, you will find a character that fits you in the pages of this novel. And, perhaps, you will also discover you're opposite.

The two main characters, Noor and Noga, come from different backgrounds, and believe in different faiths. Despite their differences, the two have a lot in common; both are strong women who stand against backward traditions in both of their societies for their beliefs.

I was blessed to meet many strong and independent women similar to Noor and Noga in the holy land. The more women demand and gain power in that region, the higher the chances for peace to be achieved.

The book has two main messages; it wasn't written to tell who is right and wrong. This ship sailed a long time ago. If you didn't figure that out yet, I advise you to keep on digging and spend some time reading, because in this age and with all this technology, ignorance is a choice.

First and foremost, the book will share with you what people in that part of the world look for. It will discuss their dreams, ambitions, goals, and of course, the many hardships they face daily.

The second message this book holds is that care and love can be found everywhere in Palestine. It might sound different than the norm, but it still can be found. You can feel love when a grandfather prays for his grandchildren in one of the many holy sites to return back home safe. Joy is noticed when children play barefoot in refugee camps even if they played with broken toys, and passion grows among young teenage boys who impress girls resisting the occupation, and standing in the face of the oppressors.

These feelings might not be reported in the news

bulletins, but they still happen. In fact, those who live under war and siege value love and care for each other more because no one there knows when they are going to lose a loved one.

It's essential to clear one last thing—I was and will always be a proud Palestinian defending my people's rights. However, that doesn't mean that I'm against Judaism and Jewish people. We as Palestinians didn't choose the religion or the ethnicity of our occupiers, we just happen to resist and defend ourselves and identity.

I'm also proud of knowing many Jews and Israelis who are standing for the Palestinian cause despite the mounted pressure from their families and communities.

Eventually, peace can be achieved only once paths of communication open up and we build bridges with the people living on the other side of the segregation walls. The past was full of pain and suffering. End the occupation and equal human rights can prevent any confrontation in the future.

What follows is the historical background of the 2014 Gaza War.

Events Leading to the 2014 War

Different events led to the fifty-five days of the war in Gaza in the summer of 2014. Frequent, unexpected events took place in several areas in the Palestinian territories and within Israel.

Since the year 1948, Palestinians have been living under occupation. Ever since, not a single day passes by without a Palestinian getting injured, detained, or killed by Israeli forces. Palestinians tried to end this occupation and left the injustices mainly by civilian resistance but sometimes by military ones. On the twelfth of June, three Israeli settlers were kidnapped while hitchhiking beside the illegal Israeli settlement of Alon Shvut in Gush Etzion, in the occupied West Bank, as they were heading back toward their settlement in the West Bank.

Five Palestinians were killed, and three-hundred-and-fifty Palestinians have been arrested in the Palestinian territories in the eleven days following the kidnapping. The majority the Israeli forces have detained are considered supporters of the Palestinian Islamic Movement, Hamas.

The Israeli Prime Minister, Benjamin Netanyahu,

accused Hamas after seventy-two hours of kidnapping the three Israelis, while Hamas denied any connection to the incident. Meanwhile, the Palestinian President, Mahmoud Abbas, said that no evidence has proven that Hamas had kidnapped the three teenage settlers.

On the thirtieth of June, the three bodies of the kidnapped teenagers were found in an open field near a cave at Khirbet Aranava in the Wadi Tellem area in northern Hebron.

The IDF is still searching for Marwan Qawasmeh and Amer Abu Aisha, the two main suspects who might've been involved in the original kidnappings.

On the second of July, a sixteen-year-old Palestinian, Mohammed Abu Khdeir, and his cousin, Tareq, were kidnapped and dragged into a car by Israeli settlers East of Jerusalem. Israeli Police located Mohammed's charred body a few hours later at Givat Shaul in the Jerusalem Forest. Preliminary results from the autopsy suggested that he was beaten and burnt while he was still alive.

Three days later, a video was aired showing Israeli

undercover agents beating up Tariq Khdeir—who happened to be a US citizen—in a secluded area after the boy had been handcuffed and pinned to the ground.

The Palestinian President, Mahmoud Abbas, blamed the murder on the Israeli government and demanded that Prime Minister Benjamin Netanyahu of Israel condemn all sorts of violence to stop the bloodshed.

Khdeir's family received his body and refused to hold a funeral. They blamed the Israeli government's incitement for the murder. They rejected the Prime Minister's condolence message, and the visit of the Israeli President, Shimon Peres, to pay his condolences.

Daily protests started to take place by Palestinians in the occupied West Bank and East Jerusalem. Meanwhile, more significant numbers of Israeli Police and the army were deployed and mobilized, trying to stop these movements in the West Bank, Jerusalem, and other cities and towns that included an Arab population in Israel.

On the other side, rocket attacks have been launched from the Gaza Strip, and Israel responded with airstrikes within the last couple of weeks. The number of rockets fired from the Gaza Strip and the air attacks by the Israeli jets continue to increase.

The economic situation in Gaza became worse, and the unity government between Hamas and Fatah was too weak to fulfill its duties in the Gaza strip.

Hamas was still the most active party in the Gaza Strip, with no, or limited, effect by the Palestinian Authority in Ramallah or the other parties.

All the previous events took place while a hunger strike was made by Palestinian prisoners in Israeli jails, protesting against the administrative detention rule that allowed Israeli forces to capture any Palestinian anytime without providing a clear list of accusations.

All told, 73 Israelis were killed including 5 civilians; on the other hand, over 2,310 Palestinians were killed reports mentioned around 70% were civilians; over 25,000 were injured, and over 20,000 housing units were made inhabitable. After the war in 2014, nothing changed for the Palestinians; they are still living under occupation, experiencing apartheid, and watching their land being swallowed by illegal settlements to this day.

Chapter 1 (Ahmed)

They say boys grow to become men faster if life was hard on them. Life is harsh here sometimes, but what made it bearable for me was my passion for soccer. I loved playing soccer in the street with the other kids. For the longest time, this was my whole world; but my sister, Noor, told me that if I train well, someday I might have the opportunity to play soccer in a famous European league.

It will require me to travel to achieve this dream, but I'm not sure how this is possible. I never saw any of my relatives ever travel before; funny enough, none of my family members even own a suitcase since none of us has ever left this country.

Today is the first day of Ramadan, the most sacred month of the year. As Muslims, we believe that Allah honored the Prophet Muhammad with the opening chapters of the Quran. We visit relatives, sleep late, fast, and pray, because Allah loves us, and we have to show him our love back. I love this time of the year; it looks like Christmas in

American movies, but with an Arabian touch!

We also exchange desserts with our relatives and neighbors. This year, I turned ten years old. And that means I became a man. Starting from this point forward, I will go to the mosque and pray with my brothers and father instead of going with my mother to the women's section. People are always in the streets during Ramadan, and best of all, no one tells me when to sleep at night because everyone is still awake between the prayers, gatherings, and the late meal, which we call *sohour*.

Chapter 1-1 (Ahmed)

June 29th, 2014

The sun rose on the first day of Ramadan. A beam of light flashed through the small square window in the center of my room, dazzling my eyes as I took up a corner of our three-story house. I lived with my parents, three elder siblings, four uncles, and many, many cousins.

The light warmed my face and dashed away any lingering sleepiness. I woke up excited, as this was an extraordinary day—it was my first time fasting a full day with my family during the holy month!

The month of Ramadan is different from any other month of the year. Indeed, we spend long hours without food or drink. Still, at night, family members pay visits to each other. It's the only month that no one forces me to sleep at a particular time, and exceptionally from the rest of the year, I don't get punished for playing with firebombs and flares in the neighborhood.

This year, Ramadan started during the three months

of summer vacation, which made it twice the challenge because of the heat, but also double the fun.

I grabbed my towel and raced through the hallway to the bathroom to prepare myself, excited about the idea of going to the bazaar later in the day. My family, and many others, would be there today on the first day of Ramadan to buy groceries and necessities for the whole month.

Because there is not enough fuel to run the power plant due to the blockade, the water was cold as usual, which compelled me to take a quick shower. Once I was done, I walked toward the living room and noticed it was unusually silent. With so many relatives living together in a tiny building and a crowded neighborhood of Shuja'iyya located on the eastern side of the Gaza strip, this was not normal. The only sound came from the clock ticking away on the wall. It was seven in the morning. I guess everyone was still asleep.

To not wake anybody, I walked carefully by tiptoeing over to the corner of the room and sat beside the Egyptian-styled furniture that hadn't been changed since before I was born.

"We've had this couch since the Egyptians governed Gaza in the 1960s." My parents were fond of telling me and I believed them. I have even seen photos from the days of my parents' wedding of people sitting on the same living room set! Actually, not many things have changed in this house since my parents' marriage. We had the same wallpaper, decorations, tea sets, chinaware, carpet, framed phrases from the Quran—in fact, I think the only additions to this house were my siblings and myself.

Somehow, this was the story of this place; I don't believe that anything changed in this country as a whole. All I hear people talking about all the time is the wish for the whole situation to change and for their lives become better. People around me always wish for things to change in this country. Maybe if this never happened, I may see some change in our house too.

I sat in the corner, staring at the only photo on the wall, a black-and-white image of my grandfather, his *keffiyah* hanging on his shoulder. Other photos of my grandfather hung in each of my three uncles' apartments, but theirs are in color. Not ours, though, and I thought maybe it was because of my father, Esam, who is the eldest. Also, they didn't have colored cameras when he first moved here. Or perhaps it's just that he liked this shade—everything in our house is grey.

I don't think that my father is alone in enjoying this color—most of the walls in the neighboring buildings are grey. Shops, banks, kindergartens, mosques—everything here is grey!

I walked around the living room, I noticed a drawing that I made a week ago about playing soccer, which I pinned to a wall at my father's grocery store to add some color to his place and his life. But it seems that he didn't like my painting; perhaps that's why he brought it up here again.

My father owned the grocery store at the bottom of our building. Whenever I would go there, I would rarely see any customers. I always found him sitting among piles of cigarettes, soft drinks, and canned food. The radio that looked like a shoebox was always either on the news or music from the 1960s.

I hadn't seen my father that morning, but it was still easy to notice his presence. When the house was filled with the earthy scent of freshly cut tobacco, I would know my father is home. Whenever I would see him coming back from work, I would greet him by bending down to kiss his rough hands; it's a way that I was taught to show my gratitude and respect for his hard work.

I don't remember seeing my father ever take a single breath in his entire life without the smoke of a cigarette coming out of his mouth. I once asked my mother whether my father sold as many cigarettes as he smoked, and she giggled and told me never to say that in front of him. Only later, she came back to me to tell me that she feared he didn't sell as much he smoked.

I noticed my mother sitting over a praying mat from behind the dining table, where she had been reading the Quran. It's ubiquitous to find women looking for an isolated corner to pray. This is something that I have witnessed my other aunts doing many times before. It's said that if you pray after dawn alone, you become closer to God, and He will hear your prayers. However, my mother once told me that this was the only time that she could have for herself.

She noticed me sitting in the corner of the living room and gave me a sweet, warm smile. When she reached me, she raised me to her lap. She said, "Happy Ramadan,

Ahmed. Come here, you early bird."

My mother's name is Etimad, which means dependable, and befits her character. Yesterday, for example, she finished all of her daily housework, helped me with my homework, helped my dad with some work at the grocery store, and looked after my three elder siblings who were enrolled in university. She made homemade jars of a traditional smashed pickled pepper and of grape leaves for my father to sell and, best of all, she found time to play with me. My mother told me stories of Prophet Mohammed, his followers, and other prophets, such as Jesus and Moses.

Last night, I helped her prepare *sohour*, a special, traditional meal mainly consisting of honey, white cheese, and some people have egg on the side. It is believed to grant strength to fast the day after and do your duty toward God. We only have it during the time of Ramadan, just before dawn, before the whole day of fasting ahead of us.

Just like these days last year, while bringing the dishes out to set the table, my mother told me, "You will be ten years in the following Ramadan. Next year, it will be for you to fast for Ramadan."

I nodded my head even though I didn't understand what "obligatory" meant.

Then she had added that "if you fasted for the entire month, Allah would forgive not only the sins you committed during the previous year but also for an extra year."

I wore a big smile on my face. I'd known it meant that God would forgive me for stealing *noga*—a type of toffee candy—from my brother Sharef.

My sister, Noor, walked into the living room, kissed mother on the cheek, and wished us a happy and healthy Ramadan. She was in her final year at the Islamic University of Gaza, studying social sciences, but she kept saying that she was a "social worker and justice fighter." I guess that is why she was on her laptop or smartphone all the time.

Noor was a big fan of a famous singer from the Gaza strip named Mohammed Assaf. The superstar won the popular TV show, *Arab Idol*, a few years ago. Every time Noor saw a photo of the singer she would say something like, "Mohammed looks like my fiancé, Sami." No one except her saw that they looked alike, but I used to agree with her only to please my sister.

Sami lived with his family at the end of our street. He worked in an international organization that provides medical equipment to the Gaza strip. Before that, he used to introduce himself as a "Human Rights Activist" as well. I used to believe that this might be an exciting job for me in the future—I hope it pays well.

Noor asked my mother to invite Sami and his family to our *Iftar*—the evening meal—within the first three days of Ramadan. My mom responded by saying, "The three days were booked for family members, but they can come at the end of the week."

My mother and Noor went to the kitchen. After ten minutes, my mother called me to check if my brother Mahmoud was awake. They wanted him to grab some groceries and necessities for today's *Iftar*.

I knocked on the door, and then checked to see if Mahmoud was awake, but he wasn't in his room. I informed my mother.

She closed her eyes, raised her head toward the ceiling, and let out a big sigh. "May God bless him and keep him safe."

Chapter 1-2 (Ahmed)

Having no electricity was part of my daily life in this city. And since there wasn't a lot for me to do in the house, I attempted to sneak out without my mother noticing. I quickly put on my sneakers and ran as fast as possible down the stairs and into the narrow street.

My cousins were already outside, dividing themselves into two teams to play soccer. I ran into the middle of the game to involve myself. While all of them fought to play as strikers, I argued to take my position as a goalkeeper.

I always admired Cristiano Ronaldo, the Portuguese national forward . He is my biggest idol. Maybe someday, I could meet him.

I took off my sneakers and used them to mark the goalposts, and stood in the middle of my imaginary nets defending it. Playing without a proper net was confusing. Almost every time someone kicked the ball toward the imaginary goal, we fought to decide whether the opposite team scored or the ball missed the target.

While we were playing, a strong and massive hand grabbed my shoulder. I looked up to find Mahmoud looking at me with a kind smile. Mahmoud is one of my cousins playing on the opposite team. He used my distraction as an opportunity to gain a sneaky advantage and shot at the goal, but Mahmoud blocked the ball and then kicked it away, winking at me.

Mahmoud said with a smile on his face, "Does your mother know you are playing barefoot in the street?"

"There is no electricity, and I heard the kids playing, and it is the summer break," I said.

He responded, "So she doesn't know, does she?"

"No, she doesn't."

"Then let's go back home."

I jumped up and down and yelled, "Come on, please! Just for another half hour, please."

My brother replied, "Okay, but you will come with me to the mosque for prayers and to the market later to grab some special items for Ramadan. That way, I won't be lying if I say that you were with me." He glanced at my bare feet and said, "And put your sneakers on. Mother will yell at you if she saw you like this. I will go to the *hamam* (men's public spa) for a bit and come back for you." Mahmoud walked away a few steps and turned back with a smile on his face. He said sharply, "Put your sneakers on. I'm serious!"

After an hour, he came back wearing new clothes, smelled like cologne, and used a small piece of *miswak* to clean his teeth. I left the game and walked with him side by side. I liked it when he looked neat. My brother is a handsome young man in his third year in the faculty of commerce, with a solid, muscular body. However, sometimes he used to smell like dirt, and I have no idea why.

We entered the mosque, where he greeted many people, patted their backs, and wished them a happy Ramadan. He asked me to sit as he went to call for prayers. It was more like an announcement for people to come and join in prayers. Once he started calling for prayers, everybody stood still. It was a habit when the call to prayer was recited to stop what you were doing, but I liked to believe the hidden reason was my brother's incredible voice. Many men used to ask Mahmoud to lead the prayers due to his delightful voice, but Mahmoud politely refused and gave the honor to one of the elders to lead the prayers out of respect.

Men from the neighborhood gathered, mostly wearing white. They stood in rows and held their hands over their chests, listening to the Imam reciting the Quran, the Word of God.

After the prayers, Mahmoud stood with some young men from the area. I couldn't hear the group talking from where I stood at the other corner of the mosque, but it looked like my brother was enjoying his time with them since I noticed him laughing.

Suddenly, a young man came running into the mosque. Instantly, the sound of laughter halted, and the group next to where my brother was standing got closer to each other. A few moments later, they all left quietly save for my brother—he remained in his place, but his mind was somewhere else.

Mahmoud was staring at nothing and playing with his thick beard. When he noticed me watching him, he came to me with a small smile. It was obvious even for a child like me to realize that it was a fake smile covering concerns.

He said in Arabic, "*Yallah*," which means "Let's go." I stood up and walked beside him. We walked together to the market and I sensed Mahmoud's distracted demeanor. He seemed like he was in a different world entirely. He wasn't blinking, and I wasn't even sure if he was breathing.

I looked at both sides of the same street I've walked on for many years. Nothing changed here as far as I knew. It must be after eleven because the familiar shops were already open, their owners already sitting outside. Not much was being sold except the bare necessities like bread and water.

Young men sat on the corners of the streets on plastic chairs. I heard once that this came as a consequence of unemployment. Sometimes I wondered, though, why all those young people holding smartphones in their hands didn't work as "activists" like Sami and Noor?

I looked at Mahmoud, "Why are all of these people sitting in the streets all day long? What are they waiting for?"

Mahmoud looked back at me and responded with confidence, "They wish for change, but their hands are tied."

"Wh-what can we do then to change their situation?"

"Don't worry. My brothers and I will break these chains implemented on us by the Israelis and make changes by ourselves."

"Do you think you can do it on your own?"

He responded with no hesitation, "Sure! Nobody cares about us since we've been neglected for so many years." He looked me in the eye and said firmly, "Remember, little brother, change doesn't come without hard work. There is a price to be paid since nothing comes for free. We will change things for the better, we are well prepared to confront our oppressors, and always remember the hadith that Imam Omar bin Al-Khattab said, 'Fear him, whom you hate'."

I was three years old when Israel implemented the siege on Gaza. However, we were taught that the Palestinian-Israeli conflict had been going on for more than seventy years. Millions of Palestinian refugees fled their homes in 1948 after the Zionists from different parts of the world settled in Palestine and kicked my people out from their homes. Since then, my people are living in poverty, refuge, and loss of identity.

"So then, people here should do something else besides sitting on the sidewalks, shouldn't they?"

"Sure!" he responded. "We're supposed to claim our rights, but to do so, we need to be strong and impose our conditions."

"Aren't we doing that? I keep on seeing protests all the time."

"That's not enough. Otherwise, nobody will take us seriously, and the Israelis won't give us our freedom if we don't fight for it. Everything is going to change if we show that we are strong and fearless."

We bought some vegetables and meat. Mahmoud also grabbed a big bag of flour and asked the water distributor to come by our home to fill the new water barrel he had bought two days before.

On the way back home, I realized I have never seen Mahmoud ask my parents for money, unlike Noor and Sharef, even though he was younger than both of them. I started to wonder why Mahmoud had so much money. Maybe he worked during the nighttime; it would explain why he was usually out until the early morning hours and was visibly drained when he came back.

When we walked through the front door, my mother rushed over to us and asked with a trembling tone, "Where have you been?"

Mahmoud kissed her on the forehead and both of her hands. Then he informed her politely, "We went to the mosque and the market."

"You know that's not what I'm talking about. Where have you been at night? I don't want to lose you."

Mahmoud interrupted her while looking at me, "Not now, mother."

My mother leaned her neck to the right while maintaining eye contact with Mahmoud and then put her hand under Mahmoud's cheek, as she knew she might not see him again due to what he was doing. He kissed her wrist again, and then a silence occupied the room for what seemed to me like an eternity, but in reality, it was not. The way they looked at each other could only be described in a poem. I felt the sorrow in her eyes, knowing she could lose her son at any moment. In return, he was trying to comfort her with his gaze; the comfort a thousand words long, for no living being could understand or feel what they had in mind except them. At that moment, I felt invisible in the world they were alone in.

Mahmoud walked to his room, and my mother returned to the kitchen with the bags she grabbed from me. As for me, I didn't know what to do, so I went to check on Sharef.

Chapter 1-3 (Ahmed)

I knocked on the door to Sharef's room and peeked my head in slowly. As usual, I found him studying at his desk. There had been many papers, triangles, and other weird pieces of stationery on Sharef's desk that I liked to play with whenever he'd allow it.

Sharef is a quiet and intelligent person; he spends most of his time studying and rarely has time to talk to us or go out with his friends. When he does have spare time, he takes care of the pigeons he raised on the roof. It seemed that studying was all that he knew in life.

My parents were exceptionally proud of him and his whole life, especially when he entered university with a full scholarship because of his high grades in school, which eased the financial burden on my father. We all believe that he will have a bright future.

When he noticed me in the doorway, he smiled and said, "Here, little one, come in." He tore a piece of paper from his big notebook and gave it to me. He said, "Draw something, and I will come back to see you in a little while."

I stared at his room, which was full of books and strange architectural equipment. He had a wooden plane on his desk, and a photo of a shining building hung upon the wall—so I decided to draw them both.

After a while, he returned and asked to see what I had drawn. He was pleasantly surprised and visibly impressed. He inquired, "How did you know about the Empire State Building?" He gazed up at the poster and then looked back at me. "You sneaky one. *Yallah*, we can talk while we feed the pigeons."

On one side, the roof was messy and full of pipes, water barrels, broken furniture, and on the other corner, was Sharef's enormous organized pigeon cage that held up to thirty of the birds. He unlocked the door, and I patiently waited. Sharef always made sure the cage was locked—not because he didn't want the pigeons to fly away. He knew they would return if they flew away, but also because he didn't want my other cousins to play with them. Sharef said, "Even if the pigeons were to fly away, they would know exactly how to return home."

I asked, "What is that building called?"

"That is the Empire State Building."

"Why do you have a photo of that building?" I asked. "Aren't there other, more colorful and cheerful buildings in the world?"

He responded while pouring some sesame seeds into the plate, "I don't look at it as just a *building*, I see it as an icon for change."

"How come?"

He explained, "It's an important landmark that illustrates exactly when the United States started taking its first steps towards becoming a great nation."

"Was that the first building in the United States?"

"No, this building, akin to many within the United States, was built by immigrants, and our country is full of refugees. I do hope someday we can make such a change and turn out to be one of the prettiest countries in the world! Or, as Yasser Arafat, our previous leader, used to say, 'I will turn Gaza into a new Singapore!'"

Sharef always dreamed of going to the United States

and completing his studies over there. He was always impressed by its modernity and endless opportunities. Once, he even mentioned that if he could achieve high enough grades, he would apply for the "Fulbright Scholarship," but I do not know what that is.

I became fascinated by Sharef's declaration that it would take immigrants and refugees to make our country great. "But Mahmoud was saying earlier that we had to change things by our own two hands and through being the strongest?"

Sharef stopped feeding the pigeons. He didn't seem delighted with Mahmoud's idea; he came closer to me and pointed his finger at my forehead and said, "We can change the world with this."

"What do you mean?"

"Through education, we can change everything!"

"But I keep on hearing that there is better education abroad. Is that true?"

He snapped back to continue feeding the pigeons. Sharef told me, "When I finished high school, I received a scholarship to study at Dunhill University. Unfortunately, I couldn't leave due to the blockade."

"Yeah, Mother told me. How did you feel then?"

"On the day the semester started, I knew for sure I couldn't leave. I was so upset and angry and did nothing but sleep for hours."

"And what motivated you to study again?"

"The next day, Mother came to me and gave me a fake plane ticket with a postponed date, believing that I will continue my studies in the US someday."

I asked, "How did you print this out? You don't use a computer. He responded by saying that Mom always had a way. Later, I found out that she asked one of our cousins to print it out.

Sharef put the plate aside and said, "Let's go downstairs. It's almost seven now, and the *iftar* will be ready soon!"

Chapter 1-4 (Ahmed)

When I opened the door with Sharef at my side, the lights flickered on instantly. As usual, I heard the sounds of whistling and cheering as my cousins, and everyone else in the household realized the power was back on.

My mother called and asked me to help her in preparing the table. I entered the kitchen, and she started handing me different dishes, one after the other, to be put on the dining table.

She made us *Molokai*, a traditional Palestinian-Egyptian dish that looks like dark green soup served with chicken, rice, and bread.

My mother told me once that superstition had been created regarding *Molokai*. Now, every time she prepares it, she inhales its steam while adding garlic to it, believing this will make it more blessed. She also believes that serving this soup on the first day of Ramadan will make our year more profitable.

We all gathered around the dining table, except for

Mahmoud, who went to call for prayers at the mosque again; as a committed Muslim, he goes and prays five times a day. We started the first meal after our fast by having a glass of water and three dates apiece before having the main dish, a tradition emanating from the great Prophet Mohammed, peace be upon him. As everyone ate, my father lit a cigarette as his main dish.

After *Iftar*, I helped Noor and my mother by returning the leftover food to the kitchen. Noor stood beside my mother, wearing her pink pajamas and bunny sneakers, and whispered to her in a kind of spoiled way that she had a favor to ask of her.

My mother gave her a firm straight look and said, "No."

Noor, spoiled, begged, "Mother, please, please, please!"

It was not long before my mother gave in. "Ugh, fine. But you must take Ahmed with you."

Noor hugged my mother and kissed her on the cheek before my mother continued, "*But*, you'll still have to do the dishes first!"

I said, "Mom, I don't want to go. Why do you want me to?"

My mom told me, "Because you are a man, and you have to be with your sister during night time. Also, your sister is still engaged to Sami and not married to him yet. Therefore, you have to stay around them."

I asked, "How come I have to stay around if they are engaged?"

My mom explained briefly as she didn't want to speak about the topic, "Well, Ahmed, they can be on their own only once they are married. Till then, you will be her little guardian."

Noor cleaned the dishes faster and more efficiently than she ever did. Then, she ran to her room and returned minutes later sporting a black *abaya*, a traditional, conservative, floor-length piece of clothing that is worn in a rush over other clothes for additional modesty and making sure that women are appropriately covered.

On our way to Sami's family home, Noor, just like any other girl in Gaza, walked as seriously and as straight as a soldier—something every girl is told to do by their mothers in order not to be criticized by the society.

When we reached Sami's doorstep, Noor asked me to wait for a second. She put on some lipstick and perfume. Sami greeted us, and my sister stopped acting like a soldier, and took off the veil from her head. Sami's mother and father appeared behind him and welcomed us inside and led us into the living room. The house was just the same as any other house in the neighborhood; simple and grey. It almost had the same decorations as we did. Sami's parents joined us for an hour before Sami's father, Essam, excused himself for the evening prayers, and Sami's mother decided to finish some housework.

Between texts and glances on their laptops, Sami and Noor talked about how they could help those who were in need by distributing Ramadan food baskets, and how to motivate people to volunteer to take the most unfortunate children to the only park in Gaza city to have *Iftar*.

My sister said, "You know, Sami, I dream of someday building an orphanage that might take care of those children who lost their loved ones. Maybe this way, I could be a value to the world."

Sami smiled, "That's the reason I love you the most because of your big heart."

He began to lean over to Noor, but she pushed him back gently and whispered, "Ahmed is here, and he can still see us and spill the beans to my Mother." I was not meant to hear her, but I did. Noor cleared her throat and looked back at me. "Why don't you play with Sami's little sister?"

"I don't like to play with girls; they play with dolls."

"Okay," Sami started, narrowing his eyes in thought. "What if you bought everyone some ice cream? That would be nice."

I perked up at the thought of ice cream. "Sure! But I need a flashlight since the electricity might cut off any minute now."

He looked in a nearby drawer, handed me a flashlight from inside, and gave me some money before I left for the grocery store two blocks away.

While I was on my way to the market, I kept on thinking about why they asked me to go to the far grocery store, even though there were two nearby stores, and they all sold the same products. The only reason I could come up with was that he wanted to tell her a secret.

When I returned, while handing them their ice creams, I noticed that Noor's hair wasn't as organized as before and that there was more lipstick on Sami's mouth than on my sister's lips. I mentioned this to Sami, and his eyes became wide. Noor giggled as he took off the lipstick and left to get some water, and my sister told me to keep that to myself once we went home.

We left shortly after, and on the way back home, I asked Noor if enemies could stop fighting and hating each other.

My sister asked, "Why are you asking such a question?"

I responded, "I heard a lot today."

"I see. Well, love can create miracles."

"How come?"

She whispered in a soft voice, "It can change people's minds and hearts. For example, you remember my friend, Fatima?"

I responded excitedly, "Yes, the one whose picture

you showed me on Facebook."

"Yes," she said. "Her father is Algerian, and her mother is French. Despite the long conflict between their countries, they found a way to get married in a time that was impossible for Algerians and French people even to be friends."

I responded attentively, "So, what difference does that make?"

"People similar to her parents made governments understand that love and coexisting can cure the hatred and grudge that had lasted for many years."

"But is there a possibility for people to forgive and forget?"

"Well, it's hard to forget, but it's important to forgive to move forward."

My sister stopped walking to stare at me, and her eyes were alight with magic when she recited the poem by Mawlana Rumi, "My friend, bestow your love, even on your enemies. If you touch their hearts, what do you think will happen?"

I thought about the poem for a minute before I felt I

understood it. Just as we could see our home, we witnessed our mother leaning out of the window, checking and looking down at the street.

"See, Ahmed? This is a message of love."

"Where?"

She pointed her finger toward our balcony and said, "Over there."

"How is that a message of love?"

"Mother kept her eye on the street to check if we are back safe. She has been doing that since I was a little kid."

I responded bashfully, "I don't like it when she does that. She makes me feel like I'm a little kid."

Noor giggled and said, "You might not like it now and consider it an overprotective act, but for me, I hope that this habit will never change. You will understand once you grow up."

Chapter 1-5 (Ahmed)

Noor and I were at home around 11 PM. My mother asked me to clean up my room and change my clothes. After a while, she came in and helped me organize my cupboard, but she was surprised to see how quiet I was.

She asked, "Okay, what's with you, sweetheart? Did somebody mess with you?"

"Yes, all my siblings did today," I told her with a shy voice.

She sounded worried when she replied, "Oh, really. What did they do?"

"They all messed with my head. They were so confusing."

"What was the reason of the confusion?"

"I was asking about the change, how things can change here for the better."

My mom seemed interested in what I said. "And what did each tell you?"

"Each wanted to change things according to how they see fit. Sharef believes that change can only be reached through education and using our brains, Mahmoud wants to change things with his own hands, and Noor said that the change must come from the heart. Who is right?"

My mother finished folding the clothes and sat on the side of the bed. "Change is a must with hard work, clear vision, and strong will."

"So, who is right among them?"

"All three of them are right. To change things, you need to be strong, think straight, and have a kind heart."

"And what if the change that you want doesn't happen? Are our lives going to be the same?"

She came closer to me, gently playing with my hair. "No matter how much time it takes," she said with the voice of an angel. "Eventually, change will happen, my love."

"What if it doesn't?"

"It's the nature of things. I promise you, dear."

"You know, Mom, there is one thing I don't want to change. I want to always be with you."

My mom was happy to hear that response, so she hugged me and said, "Yesterday, I was holding you and looking after you when you were the most adorable baby. Tomorrow you will be looking after me when I'm an old woman. Now, change your clothes before the electricity cuts off again." At that moment, I felt how comforting my mom could be. She made each one of us feel unique, yet she adored us equally. It was something I couldn't describe in words—a warm feeling that went beyond religion, sanity, sensibility, humanity, and even creation; motherhood. My mother kissed my forehead, switched off the lights, and wished me a good night.

I closed my eyes and dreamt that I was a knight with wisdom and a pure heart, who will make good changes all around the world. The first thing I wanted to start with was changing the grey color in our neighborhood to something more cheerful that brought happiness and hope into our futures.

Boom! A colossal explosion woke me up from my dream.

Chapter 2 (Noor)

I'm a simple girl living in a very complicated place.

The words I hear almost every day are those of restrictions, shame, and *nassib,* (the path God chooses for you; fate). Those three words combined are obstacles faced everyday by women when moving ahead in life.

I love my community and follow my religion and elders' traditions, yet, that isn't supposed to stop me from growing, choosing the type of education I want, and being with the love of my life. I respect the old ways, but I also try to create a way that suits me.

Chapter 2-1 (Noor)

July 3rd, 2014

I brushed my long, dark hair for almost fifteen minutes. My father loved seeing my long hair and didn't like me cutting it. It took a lot of time and effort to brush and clean such long hair as mine, but I didn't want to upset my father. I knew that Sami would understand if I wanted to cut my hair short once we moved in together.

I started to put on my clothes and wore a small amount of makeup that even I could barely notice. Later, I put on my *hijab* (headscarf). Sometimes, I wished that the whole year would turn into winter because of the different layers of clothing I wore; they warmed me up.

I walked by the living room to put on my pink all-stars shoes when I noticed my mom was on her new smartphone. She was talking to my aunt. It became a habit of my mom's to talk to my aunt in Jordan. They hadn't seen each other for ten years. But now, since I taught her how to use a smartphone, they video chat each other almost every other day.

They usually speak about everything—children, schools and colleges, cooking, how my father smoked more than he spoke; I'm happy they can call each other more often now. Only God knows when they will ever meet each other again in person.

In a loud voice, I announced, "Okay, mom, I'm leaving; love you."

My mom held her conversation with my aunt for a second and said, "Don't be late, and stay in the city center."

At that point, most of the military actions between the Israeli army and Palestinian factions were taking place in empty border areas, considerably far from urban territories.

Usually, the Israelis would kill a Palestinian on the borderline, the factions would respond, and then the Egyptian regime would mediate to stop any escalation. Similar clashes between the Israeli army and Palestinian factions are common, and the people get used to them. Usually, it would last for a day or two, but it becomes more intense if it lasts more than a week.

Due to recent events, I had decided to volunteer in one of the youth centers to provide some food, and medical kits to those considered most regrettable should the conflict escalate further. Reports showed that unemployment had reached up to sixty percent and poverty up to eighty percent.

It took me an hour to reach the distribution center. Today, it was more crowded than usual, and there were many boxes to deliver, yet more people were requesting aid. From what I saw, not everyone would go back with a food package.

I took my place at the front to register the beneficiaries and collect data with three other young ladies while the guys shelved, distributed, and handled all the heavy duties. I wanted to assist physically, but I was assigned a desk job. Despite our different roles, we were determined to help as many people as possible.

After four hours, I decided to take a break. One of my new female colleagues decided to join me for lunch; it was her first time volunteering, and she seemed friendly and eager to make friends. We sat on a bench at the corner of the distribution center under the shade of an orange tree. She attended the same university as I, and she was in her fourth year to become an Arabic language teacher, but she seemed to be in her mid-thirties.

I asked curiously, "Why did you choose a major in education?"

"Well, that is the only major my husband was comfortable with. He didn't want me to work, but he has no restrictions over me to complete my studies."

"Did you go to school after your marriage?"

"I was married when I turned eighteen just after I finished high school, and I signed up for the university program after five years of having my second child."

I was genuinely impressed. "Good for you! That certificate is an investment for your future."

She responded, "Thank you. It will also benefit when I help my kids with their homework and education."

"So, you have two kids. Did I understand that, right?"

She told me in detail, "Yes! They are ten and nine years old, and they are the world to me. I told my husband I don't want to have more children until I finish my education at least, and he was fine with that decision. Good thing we have two boys; otherwise, he would have kept trying till we have a boy."

"How did you meet your husband?"

"As everyone does here," she replied. "My mother-in-law saw me at my cousin's wedding. She thought of me as a fit wife to her son. They came to propose a week after, and here I am, married and with two boys now." She smiled and asked, "What about you? Are you committed to someone? You seem to be a pretty girl. I have a few male cousins who are looking for a bride."

"Oh, no, thank you. I'm happily engaged. I just forgot to wear the engagement ring today."

"Oh? That is nice to hear. Is it an arranged marriage, or did his mom see you in an event like what happened with me?"

Embarrassment flushed through me as I said, "Actually, we fell in love, and we went through hardship before we got engaged, but it all went well eventually."

Excitedly, she said, "That is amazing! I love hearing such unique stories. Tell me all about it!"

I explained to her, "Well, we met in a bookstore through a mutual friend. Then, he added me on social media platforms. I started to check some of his posts; they were exciting and deep. Shortly after, he started commenting on some of my posts. In a way, he caught my attention. He texted me for the first time a couple of weeks later. He didn't say anything yet, but he gave me a hint that he was interested in me. We both knew how it would go and the limits drawn for us by society."

"Aw, that must be hard on you, but it's also sweet. How long did it take him to propose?"

"Well, after four months of texting each other, Sami proposed to me, but my father refused him since he thought Sami wasn't qualified enough. But the real reason for the refusal was that Sami is a refugee from Ashdod, whereas my father is natively from Gaza."

"Yeah, it's unfortunate that some people still consider these types of differences for the moment. And was it hard for both of you to keep in touch after?"

We used to meet in the main public library, *Rashad Al Shawa,* and pretend we were looking for books. But one day, we decided to sit and have a cup of coffee in a café far away from where we lived so we could talk about it. Unfortunately for us, by pure coincidence, my cousin happened to be there and informed my father."

"Oh, God, that must've ended badly."

"Yeah, by the time I returned home, my father had already been waiting for me. He said, 'Noor, come here!' and I timidly entered the living room with my head bowed to the ground, both my arms crossed over my notebooks.

"Shivering of fear, I responded, 'Yes, Father?'

"I looked across the room, and the whole family was sitting as if we were situated in a courtroom. My father inhaled a long breath from the cigarette in between his fingers and said, 'Noor, I will ask you once and once only: have you, or have you not, been with Sami, the son of Hafiz?'

"I must've known he already knew because, rather than try to keep my secret contained, I raised my head with pride and spoke with confidence, 'Yes, I was with him.'

"Silence occupied the room for what felt like an eternity. Then, finally, my father began pacing in slow steps before abruptly stopping right before me and slapping me across the face. 'How dare you to say 'yes' this easily to my face! What do you want? Do you want to bring shame to the family and me?'

"I fell to the floor, and my mother was immediately beside me to protect me from my father. My two elder brothers had sprung into action, too, trying to stop him from slapping me again. My poor little brother, he was only eight at the time, clutched to the sofa without knowing what to do.

"'I didn't do anything wrong,' I yelled with a face full of tears. 'We were sitting in public, in the daylight. I'm dressed properly according to our religion and traditions, so how can I bring you shame?' By the time I was done, a big red spot had appeared on my check.

"'You aren't allowed to leave the house, even for the university,' my father said. My mother helped me up and to my room, preventing the situation from escalating anymore. I don't recall my father ever laying a finger on me. My mother told me later that this had been the first time he had hit any of us.

"For the next couple of days, the house was quiet and gloomy. I stayed in my room—without my smartphone or laptop—for what seemed like weeks, speaking to nobody except Mother."

My coworker nodded sympathetically. "You poor thing. And how did you and your lover end up together after all of that?"

"Honestly, I was so worried for myself, Sami, and that my father wouldn't change his mind. However, ten days later, my father asked me to sit beside him. Father began by saying, 'I talked to Sami's father earlier, and he said that Sami understands where his mistake was in a situation such as this. He has acknowledged that it's not acceptable to meet someone when neither of you has any official relation or work relations.' After inhaling a big breath of his unending cigarette, he continued, 'His father proposed once again on behalf of his son, and I refused. However, your brother Mahmoud convinced me to accept, and I give you my blessing if you still want to accept him as a husband. So, do you want him as a husband?'

"I was shocked. I didn't know whether to smile or cry, so I did both simultaneously. I felt that I won a trophy after a whole lot of hard work. I then hugged my father. 'Yes, I do! Thank you, father. And Mahmoud—' I turned to search for my brother. Mahmoud, my brother, was standing at the door, gripping his cup of coffee and smiling.

"I ran to him like a small child, jumping into his huge body and hugged him, 'I knew you had a big heart beating somewhere in this solid body of yours,' I said. 'You just don't like to show it.'

"'Those were hard times for me, but now that I have been engaged to Sami for the last six months, I am happier than ever."

My coworker appeared equally touched and taken by my story. "This is something you don't hear every day here. It sounds like a soap opera!"

My coworker looked right and left to make sure that no one was around before asking, "After your engagement, did you happen to…you know?"

I blushed and responded, "Absolutely not! I won't take it that far before marriage."

She looked at me as if she did not believe me.

I responded, "Well, we had a few of these moments. We usually check the area, and then secretly we steal some kisses. Sometimes we get a little bit intimate.."

"Where would you meet?"

"Well, we can't do anything in my place or his because they're packed with people all the time, and there is always someone watching, so we usually sneak into fire exit stairwells just like what happens in Arabian romantic Dramas."

"Is that your favorite spot?"

"Well, there was this one time where we came back home, and no one was on the rooftop of his place. We immediately started undressing each other behind the pigeon cage. It felt wild, scary, sexy, and exciting. Despite his initiation, we did not go further than second base, though, because you know we are not wed yet."

My coworker smiled at me. However, she had a hint of regret in her tone when she said, "I took the easy way, but you took the more rewarding one. I hope your love will grow and blossom. Now, let's go back to work."

Her words were sweet, but her face showed a little bit of sadness. The way she responded and how she walked back to work, I could tell she was missing passion in her life.

Chapter 2-2 (Noor)

Just fifteen minutes before the end of my shift, I noticed that my friend, Marwa, was in the distributing center preparing a news report.

I walked over and greeted her. "Hey, Marwa, nice to see you."

She replied happily, "Nice to see you, too. What are you doing here?"

"Well, I'm volunteering."

"That is so nice of you. Are you finishing anytime soon? If you are, I will drop you back home."

"I will be done in fifteen minutes. Why don't you have *iftar* with us? We haven't seen each other for a while."

"Well, you know, I still have to do some work and...."

I interrupted her, "Oh come on; you are always working, and also, I want to show you my wedding dress."

"Sure, fine, I will wrap up then and complete work

tomorrow; we are recording background clips."

I met Marwa for the first time in high school in the English club. She was interesting. Somehow a rebel at every level—her clothes, thoughts, and standards—and, without doubt, she was one of the strongest young women I have met in Gaza. Marwa wasn't afraid of expressing her opinions and thoughts. She spent a lot of time reading and researching, and she was the reason I met Sami, the love of my life.

The only thing she feared was expressing and sharing her feelings; she didn't want to be seen as a vulnerable person. She always wanted to appear as a strong and independent woman, although she shared some of her feelings and problems with me sometimes; maybe that's why we became best friends.

After work, we went to my family's home. My mom saw us first and said, with a surprised tone, "Oh, I see that you have company. Hi, Marwa!"

"Yeah, mom, I haven't seen her for a while. We have a lot to catch up on; we will be in my room 'till *Iftar*."

"Sure, hon, I will inform you half an hour before so you can help us prepare the table."

Other than Sharif, my family members weren't big fans of Marwa. They believed that she influenced me differently because she spoke her mind and didn't put on a scarf; Sami thought the opposite.

Marwa sat on my study chair while I took off my *hijab* and sat on the corner of the bed.

"How is Sami doing?" she asked.

"Well, he is so busy with everything that is happening."

"I bet he is; when was the last time you guys went out?"

"Well, I went to his family home on the first day of Ramadan, but the last time we went out was almost a month ago."

Marwa replied sarcastically, "Well, I'm happy that you stopped pretending to walk into him in the street as if he was a stranger."

I retaliated in a mocking tone, "Not everyone's parents are as open-minded as yours."

Before getting engaged, we used to walk on two

parallel sidewalks, acting as if we didn't know each other. However, we would turn our heads to see each other while walking. Our expressions gave everything away, though. It had been evident we wanted to run into each other's arms, but we had to be careful not to be noticed by the neighbors. Maybe when love is forbidden, it makes it more desirable.

She smiled and said, "Cheesy, but I hope that you are happy."

I responded with, "I'm happy, but love isn't my only reason to marry Sami."

"So, what is the other reason?"

"I won't lie to you; all the women here want to get engaged because it's the only way out of family custody. It's our only hope of freedom by society's standards. We as women do not doubt that we are just moving from one guardian to another, but I hope that Sami—my future husband—is going to give me more space and freedom than what we had before marriage."

Marwa said, "In the West, marriage might be considered a way to reduce your freedom. Here, it might be a door for more freedom; ironically, that is true."

"I don't want to break the rules and traditions of society, Marwa. I already went through a lot to marry Sami."

"You will be married, and you aren't twenty-four yet; you will spend the rest of your life with Sami. Maybe you were lucky since he is a nice guy, but others aren't as lucky as you."

"I feel I made the right choice; besides, you were the one who introduced him to me." I added with excitement in my voice, "Come on, help me in writing the marriage vows."

Marwa responded with a sarcastic smile, "Sure."

Excitedly I added, "But, before, I want to show you the wedding dress!"

I took out a big box from my closet and placed it on my bed.

"Are you ready to see it?"

She responded with a calm smile while playing with her short hair, "Sure!"

The dress was so big that it covered almost the entire bed. I kept touching it while Marwa watched from a distance, and I told her, "you know the dress won't bite you. Come and touch it."

She hesitantly touched it gently, and shortly she held the dress and sighed.

"Okay, Marwa, what's wrong?"

Marwa let go of the dress and said, "Nothing."

"I know you. Nothing makes you sad unless it's a big thing; start talking, girl."

"Well, between my work and my studies, I don't have much time, but recently, there is this guy I met. He is interesting, but it will never happen because he is married."

I interrupted her and said, "What married man? Who is he? Tell me everything now!"

Chapter 3 (Tony)

Traveling for work is an essential part of my job. Both my Italian and US passports are full of stamps of places I never thought I would travel to. What I've learned is that if you travel a lot, you see and absorb a lot. However this is a very hard life style for a married man like me

The best part is that I feel satisfied and happy with what I do in my life. I might be working long hours, responding to hundreds of emails a day, and it might not pay as much, but I know that I'm doing my best so a village would receive clean water, a doctor will have enough supplies to treat his patients, and a mother will have enough food to feed her children.

As foreigners, every place has its stories and obstacles, but Gaza is unique from the rest of the world. Despite living under a blockade and continuous fear of wars, people here don't stop looking for what I call the L's: Life, Laugh, and Love.

If I have one word to describe the people of Gaza, it

is resilient.

Chapter 3-1 (Tony)

July 8th, 2014

I glanced at the calendar on my desk. It was overwhelmed with meetings and field visits, but then I realized that the 17th of *Tammuz* would match the 15th of July, which meant that the Jews in Israel would fast almost at the same time as the Muslims in Palestine this year.

This is a holy month for everyone living on the sacred land. I hoped it would bring peace, and no further tensions would occur.

By the time I finished reading an email sent by my manager, Noga, an Israeli coworker in the Jerusalem office, stood at my door. I welcomed her in and offered her a cup of coffee. Noga spoke four languages fluently—Hebrew, Arabic, English, and French. She worked in the office for a few years now, yet she had the face of a teenager.

Noga's freckles spread over her pleasant baby-face, and, like usual, her brown hair was tied in a high ponytail. Whenever I saw her, it seemed as if she dressed for comfort, not style, because her clothes were always a little baggy and drab.

"*Boker tove*, Tony," she said in Hebrew. It means *good morning*.

"*Boker tove.* What can I do for you today?" I said.

"I heard you are going to Gaza today?"

"True, I'm leaving in a couple of hours."

"Would you mind bringing an engagement gift to Sami today?" Noga was almost pouting as she said, "I wanted to give it to him in person, but he isn't allowed to come to Jerusalem because of the recent security restrictions."

I said, "Sure! Anything for Sami. I will be happy to do so."

Noga added, "We started to work with each other more since he became the head of the department."

"Are you guys close?"

Noga replied genuinely, "We always have been. Once, he bought me a gift when I got engaged to my ex-fiancé, something some of my family members haven't even done."

"I believe he has the heart of a giver; that's why he fits this job," I said. "If you don't mind me asking, what did you get him?" I asked Noga.

Noga pulled out a black embroidered dress from a bag. I was familiar with it. It was a symbol that linked the Palestinian women to the land, but it was the last thing I would expect an Israeli woman to give a Palestinian one as a gift.

She must have sensed the confusion on my face because she started to explain herself, "I know that this might not be common for an Israeli woman to give a Palestinian."

I responded, "Well, it's unusual?"

"It's from Sami's grandfather's city, Ashdod. According to their traditions, she will wear this on her bachelorette party."

"That is so nice of you. I will make sure to take it to Sami. Back to business for now. I want to ask your opinion about the latest developments."

Noga asked, "Is there something wrong?"

"No, not at all; I need to provide ideas and build an accurate plan and schedule for the medical shipments we deliver to Gaza."

"I see."

"I'm worried that some shipments might not enter as smoothly as we expected if the situation escalates."

"In a place where everything is as fragile as this, don't leave anything to chance," Noga replied.

She caught my attention. "What do you mean?" I asked.

"You need to have alternative plans for different scenarios. You don't know when and how things will escalate here."

"Do you feel things can go south?"

"I don't know, Tony, I hope not" she answered.

We spoke a little more about work. Then we had to move to Noga's office to pick up some documents and maps. Her office wall was blue, full of paintings and different types of books. I noticed two photo frames; one on her desk in which she was standing with her family, and the other of her father lecturing in a university among her bookshelves.

After discussing work matters, I gazed into the picture on her desk of her father and asked, "Is your father still lecturing?"

She held the picture and said, "This picture was taken while he was promoting the two-states solution. The students were both Palestinians and Israeli. After twenty-five years of being a university professor, he retired from teaching, but he is still promoting peace."

That is a long time to be committed to a cause, I thought to myself.

Noga stood up and started to fix both of us coffee from her small espresso machine placed beside the window in her office.

She answered while the coffee was pouring into my cup, "He wasn't always in the peace camp. In fact, he started his life in the army."

"Why did he change his heart?"

"Well, my father was five years old when he moved here. He lost his father in one of the concentration camps, and my grandmother raised him. She was told that no one was living in Palestine and it's safer for Jewish people to move there than staying in Europe at the time." Noga gave me a cup of coffee and continued, "They spent their first years in isolated settlements from the Palestinians, or as we call them, Kepots. They had no contact with the native people. In the beginning, my grandmother found it challenging to communicate with other Jewish groups in the settlements since she didn't speak Hebrew. She was Hungarian, and most of the settlers were either Polish, Russians, or Germans." She took a sip of her coffee before saying, "My father joined the army the moment he turned eighteen. He wanted to prove that he belonged to his community and didn't want to appear as an alien to this newly born state."

The more we talked, the more curious I became. "When did your dad leave the army?"

Noga responded, "After the 1967 war, he didn't speak a lot about it. Since then, he folded his uniform, packed it in a box at our ceiling with the medallion that he earned, and we never saw them again. Since then, he changed and devoted himself to promote peace."

"Do you think that peace will ever happen between

Israelis and Palestinians?"

Noga responded, sounding skeptical, "As you know, because of the checkpoints and the walls, Palestinians and Israelis don't see or normally engage with each other without tension accruing between them. How can we make peace with people who we don't see? My grandmother and father were stuck in the settlements and didn't engage with the native people of the land, and the result ended with my father finding it easier to fight them than dealing with them. As you see the Palestinians are still here, and maybe if we approached them, we wouldn't reach this point."

"Do you think it's easier nowadays for the newer generation to create some sort of communication and connection that the previous generations failed to do?"

"It's more complicated than that."

"Why?"

Noga pointed at a painting of a young lady spreading seeds into a field on the other side of the room and said, "I bought it six months ago when I started working for this delegation from a painter's art gallery in Ramallah, in the West Bank."

"That is a nice painting."

"Every piece of art, song, or poem that Palestinians create is about their land."

"So no, there is no peace because of the Israeli settlements in the West Bank?"

She took a sip of her coffee, crossed her feet over each other, and looked up at me. "The way they taught us history at school was designed to prevent us from accepting the humanity of the other. It was deliberate and carefully constructed to keep a wall between our two people for future generations to prevent us from seeing how similar we are. The governments made us fear one another, creating walls in our minds before building real ones on land."

"But how was the situation when Israel occupied the West Bank and Gaza? There were no walls then?"

Noga took another sip. "After 1967, Palestinians started to work in Israel with no or limited restrictions. Work and business generated normal relations between them and us." Noga took another sip and continued, "I do remember when I was a child, my parents would take my younger brother, Ariel, and me to Gaza, where we would enjoy the beach. My parents would go to one of the many seafood restaurants and order a spicy fish dish called *Sayadia* while we visited Gaza's grand market and bazaars since goods were cheaper over there. My dad used to have some scholars come to our home. Don't get me wrong, there were some clashes here and there, but there was hope. Unfortunately, this didn't last long."

What Noga told me made me realize that there was a time when everyone used to get along, something I can't picture happening nowadays.

"Do you believe that they have as much right to this land as you do?"

"Well," she responded hesitantly. "They are part of this land's history, that is a fact, and no one can deny that. My ancestors, too, were here thousands of years ago. No one must be denied claiming their right to this land."

Even though she supported Palestinian human rights, it seemed to be a diplomatic answer to hear, which reflected the emotional trouble in her heart between her beliefs in human rights and her heritage.

Chapter 3-2 (Tony)

I left the office and went for a drive through the streets of the ancient city of Jerusalem. I kept thinking about what Noga said earlier today.

Eventually, I found myself at the top of the Mountain of Olives in East Jerusalem, and I parked my car close to the Seven Arches Hotel, a well-known Arab monument in the city. I went for a stroll to enjoy the cool breeze that touched my face then. On top of the mountain, time halted. The only thing that broke the peaceful silence was the call to prayers once the sunset began and the last ray of the sunlight reflected over the golden Dome of the Rock.

No wonder King Hussain of Jordan had property over here; its scenery is majestic and stunning. The breathtaking view showed the town from above as if it were a colorful historical puzzle. Every area is linked in some way to a nation or religion. Arminian, Jewish, Islamic, African, Central Asian, and Christian neighborhoods and hundreds of holy sites surrounded the masterpiece in the center—Al

Aqsa Mosque.

I didn't have any commitment that night, so I decided to drive around and check to see what it would be like to see the city from the Israeli side. I walked back to my car, started the engine, and went all the way to the other side of town, where the Hebrew University campus was based on the mountain slopes in West Jerusalem.

From above the city, I marveled at the new view and reflected on the other one. From the top of either mountain, people's contradictory perspectives weren't revealed. The city below simply lay in perfect harmony. Seeing things from above could indeed be tricky and manipulative. The peaceful scene from above didn't reflect the complex feelings that residents held to each other in the city streets and alleyways.

Everything that divided the city, segregating east from west, allowed for tension and grudges to build over many decades. Surveillance cameras were located in every corner.

I noticed that some raids took place in Sheikh Jarrah from above the street I was driving through. After evicting

Palestinians from their homes, new settlers just moved there. I heard the new Jewish settlers were from Brooklyn.

Last week, I was caught up in one of the protests on the street. Israeli military police used clubs and guns against young men who stood entirely unarmed, except for the anger in their eyes and a strong belief that they had nothing to lose.

Whenever I encountered such protests, I felt sorry for the young men who felt mistreated and forgotten.

I understand that the Israelis demand to live in peace. It's a just and reasonable request. It's essential for people to feel safe. But I also understand the Palestinians' demand for fundamental human rights. They are denied basic rights, such as equal share of water, building houses, and not being evicted from their homes. Palestinians are detained and sometimes killed for little or no reason at all.

Palestinian, Israeli and international human rights organizations described how the Israeli government dealt with Arabs in Jerusalem in a systematic approach to empty the city of its Arab residents. I had seen that with my own eyes; it's something I couldn't deny, but we can't speak publicly because my organization's narrative is to remain neutral.

Just then, my phone buzzed. It was a text from François. He asked me to join him for a drink at the American colony and look over some paperwork. I told him I would join him shortly.

The American colony is located about a fifteen-minute walk from the Damascus Gate. It was the former palace of the governor during the Turkish ruling of the city during the Ottoman era. It was later transformed into a Christian charitable community before being established as a hotel in 1902. The building resembled the scenes of English colonization in foreign countries. The structure is composed of bone-white bricks, with pillars decorated in oak. A garden outside surrounded the building and looked like a green oasis of palm trees and exotic, tropical flowers—probably imported from a land far away. Somehow it looked like a scene from *Lawrence of Arabia.*

Once I reached the hotel, François was there, sitting in the corner of the garden, legs crossed, a cigarette in one hand, and a binder full of documents in the other hand.

I greeted him, and he greeted me back. Then, a few

minutes later, a waiter came by to take our order. He asked for another Sazerac, and I requested a Palestinian beer called Taybeh.

François was a senior manager at our organization, a proud Frenchman. He was well-traveled, confident, and hardworking. Even though it was 8:00 pm, his turquoise suit still looked perfectly ironed, as if he wore it half an hour ago.

We spent some time reviewing medical shipments to Gaza and the extended budget to submit due to the latest events. We also checked the security permissions from both ends of the Eriz Terminal to ease the entry of medical supplies. He also made a note to purchase some items that might be useful for sergeants if the situation worsened.

After a couple of hours, we were done with work.

François said, "In the old days, this amount of work would take days to be done. Your generation is lucky to have all this technology." François returned the documents and notebooks into his brown leather suitcase.

I found that interesting. "I guess so, but why?"

"As a starter, I wish we had laptops and cell phones when I started working in the field."

"How was it in the old days?"

"Well, we used to write every letter by hand in three different languages—English, French, and the local language of the country we were operating in."

"Didn't you have typewriters?"

"Some of the main headquarters had the privilege of having typewriters, but the majority of us wrote letters and documents manually.

"Things were a lot slower back then. We didn't have instant telecommunication tools. We had to depend on postal mail that could take days and sometimes weeks. It's mind-blowing to me how things changed in just thirty years."

Pondering that, I said, "I'm pretty sure that wasn't your main obstacle then."

François responded, "True, I voyaged across many deserts through the burning sun using lousy, noisy wagons and crossing tropical jungles through its rivers by wooden boats to reach a mobile village to convey a message."

Although I knew he had lived a life full of adventures and wild experiences, part of me still felt he was bragging. But I remained cordial. "How many missions have you done?"

"I've served in thirty-plus different countries around the globe. I did four missions here, and this is my fifth one."

"Was there something in particular that you would miss while traveling?"

Some missions were alcohol dry, and I would crave a glass of Château Latour Pauillac. They produced it in Bordeaux, the region where I'm from."

Just then, François received a tweet that showed a photo of a child whose house was demolished earlier in the West Bank this week by Israeli forces. After he checked the image, he returned the phone to his pocket.

He said, "This is too much."

"True," I said. "At least we know."

"It's not enough that we know?" he responded disappointedly.

I looked at him and said, "We could reach out to the Israeli authorities and express our concern."

He took another sip of his drink, aimed to say something, then backed up.

I paused a little bit and told him, "You don't seem to agree."

He responded sadly, "I've told you this is my fifth mission here. I took that path so many times before; the authorities will ignore the concerns and findings to hundreds of press releases and condemnation letters they received."

"It seems that the photo bothered you?"

"What bothers me is that this has been going for decades ; there were no cameras then. I hope the new generation with the technology they have in hands can do more for these children than what our generation did."

I asked, "What else can we do then?"

He pulled out a different phone from the first one, his personal phone from the looks of it, retweeted the photo of the child on the rubble of his house, looked at me with hopeful eyes. "Just retweet from a different account because we have to remain neutral on our official accounts."

At that moment, I felt that despite François's experience, wisdom, and knowledge, he had more faith in the new generation and their methods to raise awareness and change the world for the better.

Chapter 3-3 (Tony)

It was another blistering summer day. I grabbed a glass of orange juice from the café nearby before I hit the road. I was thankful that I fixed the air conditioner in my car a week ago. Otherwise, the commute would be unbearable. It usually took around an hour to drive from Jerusalem to reach the Gaza terminal. The highway that connects Jerusalem to the southern areas is in good condition, and there was rarely much traffic, unlike the roads to Tel Aviv, the capital of Israel.

On the way to Gaza, mountain landscapes bordered both sides of the road, dotted by trees of all kinds, small houses, and golden fields of wheat, which reflected the sun's intensity.

I felt hungry. That's why I parked my car around thirty kilometers from the Gaza strip near a commercial center known as Cosmos.

I noticed a few Gazans from the way they dressed; those who managed to cross into Israel. Usually, Gazans who managed to travel to Israel from Gaza tried to buy clothes, medication, and toys before returning to the besieged territory.

As for international workers who reached this point, they usually head for Aroma, an Israeli café that serves healthy vegetarian options, such as *halloumi* salad, eggplant sandwiches with white melted cheese, and roasted coffee. For me, I saw Aroma as the last checkpoint of the western-style of life that any of the delegates could reach before entering the open-air prison of Gaza.

The security rules imposed by our operations guidelines in Gaza prevented us as international aid workers from participating in most of the regular activities. For example, while in Gaza, I am not allowed to walk freely in the streets, leave the house after ten, sleep at someone else's place, wear clothes outside of a strict dress code, or go out to eat except for some certain chosen restaurants.

Sometimes, I found it hard to remain in a place without practicing what I have been used to since I was a child. Being free is an essential part of my culture—the freedom to think, act, speak. I have to put all that on halt and monitor what I say or do while I was there. However, it helped to remember that I was sacrificing some of my comforts and values to make the world a better place for future generations.

I walked into Aroma, but I was not in the mood to have a fancy sandwich, so I ordered a cup of coffee instead and went to another restaurant at the corner that served falafel.

I opened the glass door into the falafel shop and noticed a man sitting on an overused chair facing the cook. Both were speaking in Hebrew.

I asked for a falafel sandwich and stood aside to wait. I watched the man sitting in the chair out of the corner of my eye. There was something about him, something familiar. He caught me staring at him, and I noted a flash of recognition crossing his face. At that moment, I remembered: he was a merchant who provided furniture to our office. Mystery solved; I smiled as I greeted him. We shook hands and greeted each other.

We talked for a while, and I learned that he came to Israel for medical treatment. By the time my order was done, he had already refused to let me pay for it.

"No, no, I'll pay for both of ours," he said to the cook.

I looked at the cook. who laughed. "No need," he said to us.

His statement was interesting. The cook was Israeli, and the merchant was an Arab. When the cook returned to the kitchen, I turned to the merchant. "How is it possible that you live in Gaza and he lives in Israel? How do you know each other?"

The merchant smiled and responded, "In the past, we worked together in carpentry for ten years. Last week I got a permit to visit a hospital in Jerusalem for medical treatment, and on the way home, I came here to visit him and practice my Hebrew."

We talked a little bit more, and I thanked him for his hospitality and promised to invite him to dinner the next time we would meet in Gaza.

My conversation with the merchant led me to believe that the problem might come from the younger generation. Gazans under the age of thirty haven't had the chance to meet any Israelis and vice versa. The only way they've communicated with each other is through hate messages on social media.

On the way to my car, I noticed a significant number of soldiers and troops standing beside a bus station. It was common to come across soldiers in military uniforms all over Israel, but this time it seemed more excessive than usual.

The closer I got to Gaza, the more blatant the military presence became. There was an army base that looked like a beehive, with troops, vehicles, and equipment coming in and out. Yet, it wasn't until I saw the tanks and artillery that I felt goosebumps on my arms and dread sink into my stomach.

At the first Israeli checkpoint of Eriz, I provided my passport, working documents, and the approval for driving my vehicle into Gaza to the government official at the window. She motioned me forward, and I entered the hall of the Eriz terminal to finish the rest of the process, but once I was inside, I was surprised by how few people were crossing the border with me. At a glance, it appeared that most of them were likely patients with urgent needs.

I drove my vehicle seven hundred meters over

smooth asphalt from the Israeli side to the Palestinian side. Palestinians don't have the luxury—nor the right—to drive cars in Israel or the terminal, so they have to walk in a longer twisted cage full of security cameras as a symbol for entering or leaving the open-aired prison-like territory.

I reached a commercial caravan representing the Palestinian part of the border. Once again, I provided my documents, this time to a Palestinian Authority officer who took his instructions from the government in the West Bank. From what I understood, this was the only facility in the Gaza strip that Palestinian authority had some sort of control over. The officer checked his computer and returned the passport to me before heading to another caravan where Hamas officers stamped my passport. I sympathized with Palestinians in Gaza. Unfortunately, they have three governments to deal with, and none take care of them.

After crossing the border, the streets became narrower. Rather than the smooth surfaces of Israel, I drove over unpaved roads full of ruts and cracks. There are no sidewalks, forcing pedestrians, carts being dragged by donkeys and horses, and other small vehicles to move along the same route.

On the way to the office, a group of people stood in unorganized and messy lines to receive donations from the stocks of the United Nations agency. To the right of the group, a bearded man in a police uniform stood aside. He held a thick wooden stick as he watched the crowd apathetically from his motorbike.

I drove for twenty minutes before reaching Saha Square, where the primary market was located. It was similar to every other Middle Eastern bazaar I visited. The market was full of vendors selling various meats, vegetables, fruits, animals, and colorful spices. Despite it being the season of Ramadan, the bazaar was mainly empty, except for the vendors who sat reading newspapers, a few beggars roaming around, and a handful of shoppers holding half-empty bags. I've seen it before, though. Because of the ongoing economic crisis here, people were forced to limit their purchases to primary necessities.

A couple of hours ago, when I was in Israel, the scene was entirely different. Roads are paved, there are plenty of parks, and modern buildings and cafes are everywhere. Of course, the stark differences between the two territories have always existed, but this time the change is mind-blowing.

Walking from a modern Western-inspired country into an impoverished, chaotic territory, it felt like I traveled back in time whenever I went between Israel and Gaza, despite being an hour's drive.

The people's daily lives here included military conflicts, political division, and restrictions of movement and goods. The local Palestinians have limited access to electricity, drinking water, and medical facilities, and there are a limited number of professions for people to make living wages.

Gaza is an entirely different entity from the rest of the occupied territories. It's one hour away from Jerusalem, but it's centuries behind in development and infrastructure. The economy collapsed a long time ago, and unemployment has reached up to sixty percent. People have been dependent on international aids for food and medication for decades now.

On one of the intersections on my way to work, a little boy around ten years old, dressed in a blue school uniform, knocked on my car's window and tried to sell me gum.

He said to me in English, "Two for one," as the price of two packs for one pack.

I smiled and told him with the bit of Arabic I knew, "I will buy the whole box if you go back home. It's not safe to be out late." I wanted him to go home before it got dark.

He agreed, and after I gave him the money, he asked with hope, "Are you going to pass through here every day?"

"I will need to go back home to Italy someday."

With disappointment, he responded, "Of course, you can do that. You are *Ajnabi*—foreigner."

Many of the locals envied us foreigners because we could leave and come back whenever we wanted. I grew up with many privileges, and living under similar circumstances to the Gazans seemed unbelievable to me. I couldn't believe that a whole nation was banned from traveling in the 21st century.

It's unacceptable for two million people to be denied practicing their right of movement. There is no reasonable justification for such collective punishment. No one should have to live like this. I think I'm just lucky that my parents gave me birth in the right place in the world.

As soon as I arrived at the office, I asked for a staff meeting. During the meeting, the majority of the staff was convinced that no conflict could start in Ramadan. Therefore, they anticipated no conflicts to happen during such a holy month.

I heard their wishful thoughts, although I was not convinced that a holy month would prevent military conflict. Yet, I went through our contingency plans with the team in case of a military escalation.

After the meeting, I asked Sami to come to my office.

He arrived, and we reviewed some schedules. Once we were done, I opened up to him about what happened in the meeting room earlier.

"I do have a comment I would like to address. However, I don't know if this might be offensive."

Sami responded politely, "Sure, go ahead."

I, being careful to not offend him, said, "I don't understand how everybody is so confident that nothing is going to happen just because it's a holy month. I mean, I respect other ideologies and religions, but there are facts on the ground, and we can't ignore them."

"Faith decreases their fear of a mysterious and frightening future," Sami responded.

Curiously, I asked, "Will you clarify more, please?"

"It's a defense mechanism people use after going through so much turmoil. Believing and hoping that tomorrow might be better gets them through their days."

"Fair enough," I said before remembering the other reason I asked him to meet me. "Oh, I almost forgot. Noga wanted me to give you this." I handed him the gift.

Sami smiled. "Noga is a nice person. I wish that she could've come and visited. I would've invited her over for *Iftar*."

"That's nice of you."

From the door's edge, he lit up. "Hey, you should come to my place for *Iftar* tonight."

"I don't know," I stammered. "The situation might escalate, and I don't want—"

"C'mon, please? Have some faith. I will wait for you to come."

Before I could protest further, he left.

I continued working in the office until everyone else had left for the evening. Even the generator's sound was kicking on, and the distant explosions that took place in empty lands didn't deter me from my work. I managed to finish everything around six o'clock, well before evening prayers.

Reluctantly, I put on my backpack, started the engine of the organization's vehicle, and headed to Sami's place.

As I drove to Sami's place, I passed through the Sahaa neighborhood, where Sami and I had gone once to a traditional public Turkish bath called Hamam Samra. I remembered the water being so hot and refreshing. The Hamam was decorated with white and grey bricks, and there would be a masseuse that rubbed my body until I no longer felt tense. I hope to come here again someday, maybe once the conflict ended.

The buildings in this neighborhood were close to each other, which made sense because the people's ties and relations are close as well. I understood from locals that a father will build a house containing different apartments to keep his sons close to him.

The buildings were painted with graffiti of different political symbols and figures sided in Kofi font written in Arabic. I wished I could read more Arabic so that I knew what it said. Perhaps, that is something I will learn while I am in Gaza once this is over.

My eyes roamed over the old cars parked on the side of the road. The majority of vehicles in Gaza have been on the road since the '80s, so it was strange to me that the locals referred to them as *Ajans*, which ironically means *newer models*.

"The vehicles," a local man once told me, "and everything else over here, have been adapted to meet the people's needs under the blockade." Because access to fuel is sparse, some of the vehicles have been modified to run on alternatives, such as cooking gas or cooking oil!" That's a conversation I'll remember for the rest of my life—an example of resiliency and efficiency.

It takes creative minds and even more resilient souls to overcome daily difficulties with such limited resources.

I slowly drove down the street, and tried to work around the mass of people out celebrating and ambling along the unpaved roads. I noticed that the neighborhood was ornamented with small lights and decorations that took the shape of crescents and stars. Kids and parents will tie one side of the lights and decoration to their house and ask their neighbors in the building on the opposite side of the street to do the same, so the decorations would hang between two buildings above the road. Imagine how many people are involved in such activity until lights, joy, and compassion connected hundreds of buildings.

In California—where I was raised—Christmas lights are popular beyond comprehension, but they never gave me the same feeling of connection, of community, as I felt when I'm here.

I am honestly delighted and glad that people still have the spirit of celebrating the beginning of Ramadan, despite the current circumstances. I hope these lights bring some comfort and ease somehow.

I reached the neighborhood fifteen minutes before it was time for *Iftar*. However, the area was already crowded with people demanding plates of *Humos* and filling up plastic bags of a delightful and dark drink called *Kharoub*. Among the crowd, men walked with a slow rhythm, holding the traditional *Jalabia*. Some of them held the end tip of it up with one hand. They walked in the middle of the street since the sidewalks were occupied with young men and older women in traditional black clothing. They were selling fresh and dewy arugula, radishes, mint, lettuce, and a variety of pickles. Children were running amok, like the little bundles of energy they are, despite the long day of fasting. I heard that most of the children fasted when they pass the age of ten; it was a mystery to me where they found such a store of energy.

The kids noticed my presence; they ran toward me as if they spotted a celebrity and started to surround me.

"*Ajnabi! Ajnabi!*" they cried. It's the Arabic word for *foreigner*, but they sang it with a musical beat, which was sweet and inviting. While some continued chanting, others seized the opportunity to practice the few English words they knew.

"How do you do?" a little boy said.

"What's your name?" another little girl asked.

I don't blame them since they hardly saw or met any foreigners except for a few aid workers or journalists that showed up from time to time. For them, we are the folks with lighter skin, with fewer problems, that spoke funny broken Arabic, and showed up with smiling faces and nodding heads. We are total strangers. I wouldn't be surprised if they saw me as an alien with their wide, dark eyes.

I saw Sami bowing on one knee, talking to an older woman crossing her legs on a small blue mattress garnished with white roses at the front door of his house. The lady was in her seventies in a black dress embroidered with thick, red lines and a white transparent veil that barely covered her head. Her hair was visible, and her veil was different from what the younger women were wearing. The older lady seemed to be enjoying her talk with Sami.

I greeted them both as I walked up. The older woman asked Sami where I was from, and Sami told her that I was originally from Italy.

"Yes, good people. He is welcomed as long as he isn't American."

Both me and Sami looked at each other with a smile, and he said, "Yeah, sure!"

We spoke with her for a few minutes before excusing

ourselves to walk up the stairs to Sami's place. I entered, took my shoes off beforehand, and met his parents, fiancé, Noor, and Sami's five siblings. They all greeted me warmly and asked me to feel at home.

Sami walked me to the dining table, where they prepared an enormous feast centered around a traditional Palestinian dish called *fata,* made of rice, Shrake bread, nuts, and served with chicken or lamb.

Sami filled my plate first, as his mother filled my cup with the dark juice I saw outside, and his father passed the yogurt to me. Among the three, I didn't know who to respond to first, but it was a warm, albeit sometimes confusing, hospitality that included many hand movements, Arabic words that I didn't get, and customs I'm still learning.

While eating, Sami's younger sisters didn't stop looking at me, talking to each other, and went on giggling. When I looked at them, I smiled and waved, but that only made their giggle fits worse.

After *Iftar,* Sami, Noor, and I went to the living room and had Arabian light coffee with cardamom—Sami told me it contained more cardamom than coffee since he knew that

I didn't drink coffee late at night. Then, I turned to Noor, who was on her phone at the moment, and I couldn't help but ask her about how the social workers and activities came along.

From her laptop and smartphone, Noor showed me examples of different projects she participated in with her friends to raise awareness on different social justice topics. They posted articles, photos, and videos on various social media platforms. Noor and her friends tackled different issues from living under occupation, blockade, child labor, women's rights, gender equality, poverty, injustice, rights to speech, and other criticisms of Hamas' way of controlling the Gaza strip.

Suddenly, the room went dark. Blackouts weren't unusual to occur. Not a second later, a small electric lid attached to the wall lit up. Sami left the room to turn on the generator, leaving Noor and me alone in the dark room except for a small light on the corner that happened to shine on Noor. Noor was wearing a blue pair of pants and a long sleeveless shirt with a petulant beret.

I reached for the glass of water that I could barely see in front of me.

I wanted to break the ice by saying something, "Sami told me so much about you," I cautiously said, hoping I didn't offend either of them.

"Oh really, Tony? He told me about you too. Sometimes I get jealous of you."

"Me?" I was surprised, and I nearly spit out my water. "Why is that?"

"Sami likes working with you, and he sees you as an idol, although you were tough on him on several occasions," she said with a slight giggle.

"I see, sure, I will try to put less pressure on him," I said with a laugh.

"I understand. It's been a little bit busy recently."

"That is nice of you. When was the last time Sami took you out?"

"It has been over a few months now; you guys were busy with work due to the latest unfortunate events." Sadness flashed over her expression as quickly as it disappeared.

I tried to comfort her by adding, "I hope everything

is going to be better soon."

"It's okay, and I prefer going to the beach in the winter time anyway."

I said with a smile on my face, "Why in winter? Usually, people prefer visiting the beach in the summer."

Noor moved closer to me as if she wanted to share a secret and said in a low tone, "Usually in the winter, the beach isn't as crowded. Three months ago, Sami, his sister, Razan, and I, went to the beach near the Nusirat area, and no one else was there. That had never happened before."

"Nice! Did you guys have a good time?"

"We couldn't believe that it was real for a second. I felt that I was dreaming. Having all that space to ourselves in a place that is normally very crowded was a miracle."

"Did you guys swim or have a picnic over there?"

Noor said with excitement, "Even better, I took off my veil, allowing the sea breeze to comb my hair for the first time since I was a child. The sea was calling me, and I couldn't resist. I walked on the tips of my toes toward the ocean and let the salted water rise to my knees. God, it was the greatest feeling ever. Cold, but great."

I took a sip of water. While it was interesting how small things like this might be considered an achievement for a young, educated woman like Noor, it felt like she hadn't enjoyed her youth. Life isn't easy for women here.

"And what did Sami do?"

She smiled and said, "Well, I dared Sami to race me. Razan drew a line on the sand and stood on the other end to announce who would be the winner."

"Is that so?"

She clasped her hands in front of her chest, recalling, "We started to race, and as far as I could remember in my entire adult life, it was the first time my legs experienced running. I was hugging the cold breeze of the ocean while running, appreciating the little freedom that Sami allowed me to have in such a society."

"And who won the race?"

"I did, of course; I jumped into the air the minute I reached the mark, happy with my victory over Sami, who was way behind, pretending that he was running."

"I ran back to him and asked him why he didn't run; he responded that I'm always going to be his number one."

Noor beamed. "It was a sweet answer, but deep down inside, he knows I will beat him any day; he was running out of breath."

I worked with Sami for six months. I've come to recognize, and depend on his steady, calm personality. But Noor, she was different; energetic, and the complete opposite of Sami.

I picked my next words carefully, trying to avoid offending her. "I know this might be personal, but what made you interested in him, to believe that he was the one you will spend your life with?"

Noor said confidently, "Many things, Tony. Sami is an open-minded person. He helps people, supports me in everything I do, and allows me to grow. He has beautiful big hands that can warm mine in winter and hold me up when I fall."

The high squeal of the generator cut off our conversation. Finally, the lights returned in the living room, and Sami returned as well. "Sorry for being late. We were out of fuel, so I had to buy some from the gas station."

"No, it's fine. I had an interesting conversation with

Noor."

I spent an extra hour with Sami's family, and they kept bringing me fruits and sweets, but I left before the late-night prayers around nine o'clock. I went back to the organization's premises and checked my emails to find that the situation wasn't comforting. Something big was about to happen.

After a couple of hours, I received a phone call from Sami. "It's been named. The Israelis announced that the military operation against Gaza is going to be called the Protective Edge."

"I see…it looks like there is no going back. So from now on, we have to start working according to our emergency plan."

I hung up the phone, stood in front of the window, and checked the view of the dark city of Gaza. Finally, I lit a cigarette and sighed inwardly, imagining what would happen in the next few days and how Ramadan would look this year. A war was on the horizon. No one knew how long it would last, how many lives it would take, and how much destruction we would have to clean up when it was all over.

The smoke coming out of my cigarette was gray, wavy, and vanished within a few seconds. It reminded me of the way I looked at my old faith.

I hope that the people of Gaza would have more faith than me to overcome the pain and fear that is about to enter their lives.

Chapter 3-4 (Tony)

Tony sends an email to his staff members.

Today: 07:04 AM

From: Tony.bianchi@med.org

To: headofdep@med.org

Subject: Morning Briefing 15-7-2014

"*Dear Heads of Offices and Heads of Departments,*

<u>Military Updates:</u>

It's been a week since Operation Protective Edge took place in the Gaza strip. The air jets keep on targeting different locations along the strip, leading to many Palestinian civilian casualties.

The different Palestinian military factions continue to launch various rockets into Israel. The last 24 hours have seen a decrease in both the raids by the Israeli air force and missiles from the Palestinian military factions.

We cautiously believe that today's military events

are considered less intense than the previous days.

According to the latest numbers provided by the Ministry of Health, the death toll is 186 Palestinians since the start of the operation.

End of Report.

Regards,

Tony"

I sent the email to my staff and felt optimistic about the war reaching an end today. Both sides were holding fire, and the negotiations in Cairo were going well. I also noticed that, unlike the previous two wars Gaza witnessed, this time the Palestinians were more united. For the first time in seven years, a Palestinian delegation from different parties spoke with one voice.

It's unfortunate what the people have gone through during these hard times, but I hoped that this might be a new phase for Palestinians to work with each other.

Sami called me to say they're ready to deliver the

shipment to the hospital. I headed downstairs into the garage and made sure to hang the flag on the right corner of the vehicle—as we do in times of crisis. We drove to the Shifa hospital, the most significant medical facility in the besieged strip.

We approached them with various heads of departments in the hospital, then quickly met with the busy surgeons. While the surgeons were meeting with us, they changed out of their bloody PPEs and coats into new clean and white ones, ready to start another operation.

We took all of their notes, provided them with the equipment they requested that included most of their vital medical needs, and we promised to deliver more supplies in the next few days.

When our work was done, we returned to our vehicle, and Sami asked me to wait for him so he can attend the noon prayers at the hospital mosque. I waited in the driver's seat while Sami finished his prayers, and I noticed this was the first time in ten days that I was not working.

I was dying for a cigarette, but I couldn't go for one; Muslims are not allowed to smoke during the day of

Ramadan, and though I'm not Muslim, I didn't want to offend the locals. I'd rather wait until I returned to the office.

Today's weather was nice. The skies were clear, the breeze was gentle and complementary to the warm, but not too hot, climate. I took this as a sign that good news would come out of the negotiations between the different fighting parties.

I still heard the sounds of explosions from time to another, but I had a feeling the fighting was less intense than the previous seven days. I hoped that a peace treaty could be achieved soon.

I watched people as I waited. There were many medical staff, police officers directing traffic, injured people on stretchers and, of course, in such circumstances, journalists everywhere flittering around like hummingbirds. I couldn't help but notice a fair young lady with short maroon hair, a mic in hand, and a note with a pen in the other. She walked confidently and elegantly strode towards a tent made especially for journalists just beside the hospital's main building.

I know that woman, I think she is Sami's friend that

I spoke to a couple of times before. I never noticed how pretty she was! Why am I attracted to her now? Is it because of her confidence or is it because of how bravely she is covering this bloody war? Not sure why but I couldn't take my eyes off her. I know that I'm married and my wife is waiting for me back home; yet for some reason, I couldn't take my eyes off her! Looking at her it felt as if the war had reached an end and time itself had frozen. She was the only person I could see, and I couldn't hear the sound of the people, sirens, or explosions. Amidst everything, it had been a while since I had seen such beauty. I even thought of going near her, because maybe if she saw my badge, she would approach me and ask me for an interview. I didn't care to be interviewed; I just wanted to talk to her.

I stepped out of the vehicle, but quickly returned to my seat. I couldn't do this. I couldn't walk up to a woman and start flirting with her. It was not the time or place for such thoughts or acts.

"What's up, boss? You seemed to be lost in the clouds," Sami asked, startling me out of my daze.

I turned to him and started to get back into the vehicle. "Nothing, just stretching my legs and enjoying the sun. It's been a while since we left the office."

I paused, then finally asked, "Is it normal to appreciate beauty even in the middle of chaos and gloom, Sami?"

Sami sat beside me on the passenger's seat and said evenly, "It's almost impossible to notice beauty under such circumstances when we are trying to survive and serve those who are in need."

"So, the answer is no?"

He thought for a moment before adding some wise words, "Well, if you managed to notice such beauty in the middle of chaos, then hold to it, because it must be unique."

Just before I started the engine, Sami asked to leave for a minute, and he bounced out of the seat. I remained sitting in the driving seat to see him make his way to the journalist's tent. To my further astonishment, he started talking to the fair young journalist I had been eyeing.

I smacked off the top of the steering wheel. "Really? You're kidding me," I said to myself.

Sami returned two minutes later yet on his way to the vehicle she looked at me for a few seconds with her big pretty eyes.

For me that look could've lasted for an eternity, she stood steadily with pride, and I couldn't explain it but my whole world stood with her. Nothing was moving except for my heart which was about to come out of my chest. This lasted till she gave me a small smile, barely waved her hand to me and left the scene without waiting for me to wave back.

Jealously, but with clear humor in my tone, I said, "Wait till I tell your fiancé about this."

He innocently smiled. "That is Noor's friend," he said, shaking his head and laughing. ", I introduced you to her before, don't you remember."

I said: "I do, I do remember her. But remind me how Noor and Marwa are friends?"

"They went to school together, and both have been active bloggers, but Marwa took it to another level. Now she's reporting for international news agencies."

"I see. Good for her. Marwa is her name, you said?" I liked the way her name sounded on my non-Arabic speaking tongue.

Sami cocked an eyebrow and grinned. "Hard times

will reach an end, and the beauty will become visible again." He added sarcastically, "And yes, her name is Marwa if you'd like. Maybe, we can go for dinner some other time. But for now, we have work to do."

I put my sunglasses on and smiled sarcastically. "Sure thing, boss."

Chapter 4 (Ariel)

July 17th, 2014

I finished my last prayers before leaving for the battlefield at the Western Wall—the holiest site in the Jewish faith. The bricks of the wall have witnessed our presence in this land for two thousand years, and they will remain to observe our modern state and expanse.

Since I was a kid, I've known that I wanted to defend the Israeli heritage from any threat. Today, I'm doing just that: standing in front of evil and terrorism.

If we don't respond to what's coming out of Gaza, other nations and groups will think that we are easy prey and might try to eliminate us. We must make an example of Gaza so that others will think twice before threatening us.

Being a soldier is not easy. Nightmares haunt you, leaving you with no place to run and nowhere to hide from your thoughts. I can handle all of that and find peace with myself for being a soldier. However, my father never did, and he remained divided between two worlds.

Chapter 4-1 (Ariel)

July 19th, 2014

10:00 A.M.

Military Medical Center Southern Division

The lad's spirits were high. The only complaint I kept hearing was that we might lose a couple of weeks before enjoying summertime on the beaches of Tel Aviv. I'm not worried about that. Beaches will still be there once we are done with the trouble coming out of Gaza.

As for me, I was studying my dog tag, waiting for my turn in line for the final medical check before the battle began in forty-eight hours.

Neither my mother nor sister supported my decision to become a soldier. My mom always worried that I would get hurt during a mission to any of the bordering Arab states and territories that surrounded us and didn't want us around. My sister, on the other hand, is a lefty who believed in equal rights for Palestinians. I don't think Palestinians will give us half of the rights we gave them now if they had the upper hand.

I walked toward a vending machine to buy a soda drink in the hot weather. I pulled a coin out of my wallet, but couldn't help notice a photo of my father in his military uniform. Despite that, he changed his career to become a university professor. However, part of me would like to believe that he missed being a soldier. Once you are in the field, everything else feels unfamiliar.

My father didn't interfere in my path. He made a few comments from time to time, but he always believed that I would find my way and figure it out on my own. My dad was always divided between who he was and who he became, and I'm sure he didn't want that for me. When he first left Hungary to come to Israel, he didn't know any Hebrew and he found himself fighting alongside the first Zionists to establish the State of Israel.

Now, he is a retired philosophy professor who spends most of his time writing research papers and publishing them in journals. He is trying to analyze and observe actions rather than being involved in the action as he was before.

Nevertheless, despite his words speaking against

war, his face spoiled that he wasn't against my decision to be part of the defense forces. Deep down, he was still a soldier, but maybe my dad took another path so he could sleep without guilt.

I kept looking through the window from our conditioned barracks. To kill time, I started writing a few random words over the cold, foggy dew on the window while waiting for my name to be called. It was a sunny day outside with clear blue skies, but it wouldn't last for long, at least not in Gaza. Negotiations were taking place in Cairo, but they were reaching a dead-end; the same as our patience with Hamas. They thought they could just hurt us, and we would let it go; the Gazans don't know who they are messing with.

I heard a voice call out, "Ariel, please approach the desk."

I stepped forward, and the officer checked my military ID and walked me to the test room, where I awaited a doctor. I sat on the bed, and the room was small, but well-equipped with medical supplies. There was a picture of a bluefish centered on the wall beside me.

Someone knocked and entered a second later. The minute I saw her, I puffed, rolled my eyes, and thought I said out loud, "Oh, geez."

"Hi, Ariel, I'll be your examining doctor today. Let's be adults here and let me do my job so you can go back to your unit as soon as possible."

Out of all the people in the world, my sister's ex, Anat, was the last person I wanted to examine me. I never liked Anat nor wanted anything to do with her, since she was the person who turned my sister into a lesbian. I was never happy with most of my sister's boyfriend choices either. They were always either Lefties or Arabs, but this was another level for me.

"Once you are done having your flashback and hating me, please roll up your sleeve. I want to test your blood pressure."

"Is there any other doctor?" I said.

"Sure. I can reschedule you for another day. Not sure when we will have an appointment available, though."

I thought for a second before rolling up my sleeve. "Fine. Let's get done with this."

"Thank you."

She started the blood pressure cuff, checked my eyes, and asked me to open my mouth. She continued her examination, and wrote down numbers and details in a report.

The longer we were in the room together, the angrier I became. I did not like her for what she did to my sister, and I didn't approve of her lifestyle. Finally, I couldn't contain myself any longer.

"Why Noga?" I blurted out.

"Pardon?" she said.

"Why did you change her?"

Astonished, she snapped back, "This is not the place nor time, Ariel!"

"She was a normal girl."

"She is still a normal woman! She just discovered another side of herself."

"You could've been with anyone of your own kind. It's a free country, there are a lot of you here… changing our values."

She responded firmly, "Exactly, soldier. It's a free country, and she is free to make her own choices. Now calm down, or I will report you to your commander, and you'll get punished for crossing the line here."

I took a deep breath in, and out. After a few minutes, I said, "The thing is, she never got over you."

Anat looked at me as if she found something lost. "What do you mean?"

"She hasn't seen anyone since you guys broke up, or at least as far as I know. She even mentioned you to my parents recently. I never spoke to her about you, because I was never accepting of you two being together."

She appeared shocked at the revelation. "Wow. That is something I didn't expect to hear: that she is still into me, especially from you. Knowing where you stand about the two of us being together."

"I will never give my blessing, but I care for my sister. Why did you break up?"

Anat sat beside me. "Because I chose to accept this job, to be a doctor in the military. It meant leaving Noga behind since she refuses any participation with the military.

This was the hardest decision for me to make. I don't approve of war, but if it happens, someone must be here for those who are in need."

I responded, "If it weren't for the different wars that the military participated in during the last decades, our Jewish identity and people would vanish. We have to do what we are doing to remain safe."

Anat calmly said, "I don't participate in politics. My job is to heal people, and I won't hesitate even a second to help an injured or wounded Israeli or Palestinian, whether he is a civilian or a fighter. We, as doctors, took an oath to help everyone and anyone in need despite their beliefs, religion, or race." A moment of silence went by before Anat hesitantly, yet eagerly, asked. "How is she doing now? Is she fine?"

I didn't like the question, but responded anyway, "Don't get me wrong. I'm still devoted to my religion, values, and beliefs. Yes, we are acting as a Western country, but we are in the Middle East. Here, your faith is the primary factor for society to accept your choices and identity. Please understand where I stand comes out of love for my sister."

I stood up to put on my clothes, and we both calmed down a bit. She gave me a document to pass to my commander.

Rather than reading it, I just came out and asked her, "Is everything okay with me?"

"Yes, you are fine," she said. "You need to lose a little bit of weight, that's all." Then, she added with a smile, "Your sister was in better shape than you. I checked both of you closely, you know." Anat winked

"Oh, geez."

Chapter 4-2 (Ariel)

July 19th, 2014

09:00 P.M.

Israeli military base close to the border with Gaza

I spent the last couple of hours praying in front of a fire I built in the hearth earlier. I came across a story mentioned in the Tanakah holy book, which caught my eye. I looked out at Gaza from our camp; in an hour we were launching our attack to defend our people and state.

"In the valley of Elah, two armies were poised for battle with nothing but a hill separating them. The larger of the two was that of the Philistines. They were well-armed too. The smaller one was that of Saul, King of the Jews.

"Suddenly, a Philistine giant named Goliath appeared on the hill, and his words came roaring like thunder. 'I challenge anyone in your miserable army—king or slave—to fight in a duel with me! The victor will make his nation victorious, and the other nation will surrender!'

"Day after day, for forty days, the mighty giant appeared on the hill to repeat his challenge, morning and evening, and without receiving any reply, proceeded to mock and jeer the Jews and their God.

"Among the armed forces of King Saul were David's three older brothers, Eliav, Avinadav, and Shama. David was told to stay home to tend his father's flock. With his youthful age and poetic soul, David was not regarded as a warrior at all.

"When he came to the camp and witnessed the painful scene and the mortification of his people, he decided to take up the challenge.

"At that very moment, David let a stone fly from his sling. Swift as an arrow, it flew and struck true to its mark. The next moment, the giant's huge body lay prostrate upon the ground, his forehead crushed by the sharp little stone that struck it and pierced his head.

"David ran up to the giant and stood upon his body. Having no sword of his own, David drew the giant's sword and cut his head off.

"When the Philistines saw that their champion was

dead, they fled. Saul's armies, regaining their confidence and courage, pursued them with might and mane. It was a great and lasting victory. David, thereupon, became the greatest national hero."

When we were little kids, our parents used to read this story to us. How fearless and strong we felt then. At the time, we were outnumbered and poorly armored. However, against all odds, we won the battle, and God fulfilled his promise to our people.

There is no way we will lose this war. We are better trained and equipped, and God has always been on our side. We have the most advanced weaponry in the region, and the most sophisticated technology.

I stopped reading from the holy book, took off the black *Tefillin* I used for praying off my arm, and packed both beside an album of family photos in my backpack.

I started to paint my face with colors that matched my uniform and anger. I began to prepare myself for war and victory.

"*Shalom*, Ariel," I heard a voice from behind me say. "Hope you are enjoying the fire." I recognized the voice. He was my good friend since primary school, Isaac. "Let me help you, my friend."

"*Shalom*, Isaac," I responded. "Good to see you here. I hope you guys are ready tonight. We depend on you today."

Isaac was operating in one of the artillery units. His unit would play an essential role in achieving victory tonight. Without them, we won't be able to cross beyond the enemy's territories.

I'm proud of him, but I preferred where I was. I won't accept any other role other than being on the frontlines. I wanted to be God's sword. I wanted to embody the persona of David, and defend my people against Goliath. I've trained hard for such a battle.

Since the very beginning, I wanted to be part of the Golani brigades, the elite unit of the ground forces and the pride of the Israeli army as a whole. The first Golani soldiers were farmers and simple immigrants, yet they felt a strong connection to the land of Israel. For this reason, Golani's soldiers were designated by brown berets. The brown symbolizes the brigade's association with the soil of Israel. That's why our symbol speaks for itself: a green tree on a yellow background.

Despite that my brigade was traditionally associated with the Northern Command. We were asked to operate once again in the Gaza strip. They would let us take the lead in battles and sent us for special missions. We were called for when no one else could do the job—that's why we were considered the best of the best in the army.

"The battle will commence in less than an hour," said Isaac.

"We will end it soon," I said. "They won't last for long." I added after a pause, "I want to ask you a favor. When you start shelling, make sure the first shell you send them is the one I signed."

Earlier, when camped in the area, I had reached out to Isaac and asked to sign a shell. I wrote on the top of it: "From Ariel, with love 19/07/2014".

"I don't know, Ariel, but not all Palestinians are members of Hamas. The majority didn't ask for such a war to take place."

I avoided eye contact with Isaac and took another gulp of my black coffee. "We negotiated with them first, then we warned them and asked them to leave the border areas. They brought it to themselves."

"Maybe if we gave the negotiation talks a little bit more--"

Firmly, I interrupted, "They had their chance! They brought it to themselves. It's off the table now." My voice hardened. "Politicians make the decisions, not us. We are soldiers, and we go by the orders, so don't be soft and find courage."

Deep down, I knew that Isaac wasn't totally wrong. However, there was no reason for them to open fire on us. And then I started to think, "What do the Gazans want from us? We withdrew from Gaza nine years ago. Why don't they just leave us alone?"

I looked into the fire. I was feeding it wood to grow, and it was feeding my grudge in return. I started to convince myself that since they didn't accept the truce, everything that happened was on them now! In fact, we were considered merciful to them.

Some of their patients had been treated in Israeli hospitals. We allowed food and necessary goods to enter through our borders to their merchants. We allowed humanitarian aid to pass by. The world kept criticizing us no matter how much good we did.

We are the only democratic nation in the region, and yet the world condemns us, day and night.

The only reason we imposed a siege over them was to end their violent acts against our people. They are the ones that kept proceeding with hatred.

A call from the remote speaker tower drew my attention. *"All units take your positions. All units take your positions."*

I dumped the rest of my coffee on the ground, raised my rifle over my shoulder, and put out the fire in front of me with the hope of starting a greater one soon.

Isaac was preparing himself as well. "I have to go; they are calling us. Make sure you return in one piece," he said.

"Just make sure to keep my dinner warm. I will be back here in no time." I tried not to think about whether or not this was the last time I would see my friend. "Isaac? Don't stop shelling, even if your arms hurt from reloading the artillery."

The role of the artillery was to smooth the infantry path and allow us to enter without being targeted by snipers or ambushed cells or, worse, kidnapped. The Israeli government and the army leadership won't allow for another soldier to be kidnapped after what happened with Gilad Shalit in 2006. We believe that a dead soldier is better than a captured one.

We have seven-thousand of them in our prisons, but we won't allow having one of our soldiers in their custody; they are savages.

The plan was to isolate the Eastern side of the Shuja'iyya neighborhood and secure the area for the army to search and destroy all the tunnels that head directly from that neighborhood into the Israeli side.

I checked my luggage for the last time to make sure everything I needed was there, reloaded my IMI Tavor TAR-21 rifle, put on my *Mitznefet* helmet, and moved toward the troop carrier.

Just a few steps before heading to my line to enter the carriers, I received a message from my sister, Noga, on my cell phone. I didn't want to open the text, knowing that she had a soft heart for our enemies, yet I couldn't resist.

"Ariel, it's not too late yet," her message began. "You can make the right decision and leave. I can't handle losing you. We could support you and find a way to defend you even if you ran away from the service."

I lifted my head, stared at the pitch-black sky, and wished it would swallow my anger. How could she think this of me? I won't turn my back on my country, especially after all this time and training. Not on the day I was called in for duty. Does she think I'm a coward?

I shouldn't respond. I should load the carriers and ignore her text. But I couldn't resist. "Don't worry; I will be fine. I will make sure to bring you a souvenir from Gaza."

I locked down both my phone and heart and prepared myself for the longest night of so many people's lives, a night that a lot will keep dreaming and talking about for many years to come. The sounds of the first artillery shells began at 11:00 PM., and like everything that began, it started small but got larger with time. We weren't far away from the artillery when the smell of the powder spread all over the camp and mixed with our eagerness for payback. As a soldier going to invade a city, seeing its defences and the walls falling apart made me feel...satisfied.

Some soldiers started to whistle, others cursed the enemy while others took selfies with smokes coming out of Gaza in the background to share with their friends later. Everyone was excited to show how they participated in setting the city of Gaza on fire, how they were there when smoke started to rise into the sky.

While the fire was burning in the city of Gaza, I lit a cigarette and compared the smoke coming from my cigarette to the one coming out of the town.

At that very moment, a rare sweet breeze in hot July passed by and kissed my face like no lover ever could. It was the perfect scene of destruction for me.

Being on the top of a hill gave me the sense that we were in control of everyone's fate. We were capable of deciding to move the artillery two meters to the right or two meters to the left. We could do whatever we wanted simply because we were superior. In other words, we would choose how many would live or die that night, and just a week from now, we would go to the beaches of Haifa and celebrate our victory as if nothing happened.

I spread my arms out wide, turned my head back over my shoulders, inhaled a deep breath from my cigarette, and blew it out.

I yelled triumphantly to the sky as it filled with smoke, and was suddenly reminded of a Jewish myth. "Tonight, we will unleash the giant eagle, Ziz, and let his flames burn the ground and cover the sun's light!"

Our unit was the first in line, and it was time for us to move. We entered the troop carrier—which we called Namar—in pairs, and each sat across from the other.

I settled down then and started to chew a piece of gum. The rumbling engine ignited and the heavy metal door shut, preventing us from seeing the camp anymore. I knew the next time the door would open, it would be from beyond enemy lines in the battlefield.

The carrier started to move smoothly. The soldiers inside chatted about how they didn't have the chance to watch the World Cup matches on big screens and placed bets on who would be announced as the champion this year.

We stopped for a minute, then the carrier started to move again, and the driver called to us in the back. "One of our soldiers was going to open the gate at the Gaza strip to allow our vehicles to enter the Shuja'iyya neighborhood. We are about to cross enemy lines, so please stick to the plan. Double-check your luggage again and keep your radios on at all times."

Once the carrier pilot finished speaking, the only sound I heard was the sound of the engine and the internal air conditioning. Everything else, all the chatting, quietened.

I noticed that some of the soldiers were sweating, and I wanted to convince myself that it was because of the summer heat. But the truth was, they were nervous. I handed each of them a piece of gum to release their stress. After all, many of them had never fought in a war this big.

The movement of the carrier became rougher and slower. Then, I realized we had entered Gaza and our role in the operation was about to start.

A message from the Commander-in-Chief came across the radio, "We are engaging against Hamas and returning peace to Israeli citizens. Your nation is behind you, and terrorists from Hamas and the Islamic Jihad are ahead of you. I trust in you, and I believe in your capabilities. Go ahead and go forward. Out and over."

Two days ago was the seventeenth of Tammuz, marking the start of the *Bein HaMetzarim*—three weeks of mourning for the destruction of both the First Temple and the Second Temple in Jerusalem. During the *Bein HaMetzarim*, it was customary for us to spend extra time studying Jewish law, to give to charity, and not to hold joyous celebrations—such as weddings—or wear new clothes.

This time, it is not we who would mourn.

It is time to show them what we are made of. Now, we bring them Hell.

Chapter 5 (Mahmoud)

I'm a big, brown man with a beard. I wear a black mask to cover my face to hide my true identity, pray five times a day, and hold a rifle. To every mass media organization, we represent terrorists and savages. They never want to hear why we are doing this; instead, they add the words to our mouths with their scripts, narrations, and whatever else suits their agenda.

To be a fighter wasn't my first choice. I would rather live a normal life, have a nine-to-five job, return home to a beloved wife and sweet children, have food in my fridge, electricity in my house, fuel in my car, and some extra money to travel, maybe.

But these are only dreams. I tried to yell, but no one heard me. I gave up on every peaceful solution; that's why I hold the rifle, and *then,* they started listening to me.

They don't like what I say, but at least now they listen.

Chapter 5-1 (Mahmoud)

11:00 PM

July 19th, 2014

Gaza, under the ground in one of Hamas's tunnels

"It's time to show them what we are made of. Welcome to Hell on Earth."

These were my first words when I saw the Israeli tanks, troop carriers, and other vehicles crossing the border into our territory. We spotted them not far away from our tunnel where it was correctly located and ambushed.

I saw them clearly with my night green vision camera. They looked like aliens that we would see in movies, coming from outer space, invading in significant numbers, armed to the teeth and ready to fight with their modern tanks.

They moved slowly and carefully. Despite the protection of choppers and drones that gave them the advantage of seeing what was happening on the field from above, we could see them from under the ground. They had no idea what was going on underneath them, and that would be their demise.

Once I spotted the movement of our enemies, I was supposed to return to the hall where my three brothers-in-arms and Islam were waiting for me. So, I ran through the narrow tunnel to reach a safer area and to be as far from the tunnel entrance as possible so that I was not spotted.

Once I reached the center, I took off my mask, called our command center through the radio, and informed them of the latest developments. I reported the estimated number of tanks, vehicles, and troops I saw and provided them with the coordinates of our area. Afterwards, I sat tight, waiting for new orders so we could act accordingly.

It was 3:30 a.m., and I asked brother Sofyan to start preparing *sohour*, so we could eat and have some energy to proceed with our military duties while fasting in the day time. I asked my other two brothers to ignore the tank's movement above our heads and to try to get some sleep. As for me? I remained awake, awaiting new orders from the higher-ups.

The tunnel where we were located was twenty meters under the surface, around two meters tall, and with one-and-a-half meters' width. We managed to move in it without bending our necks too much.

Despite the siege implemented by the occupation, we managed to build tunnels that were well-finished and highly fortified. It was built out of cement and iron and wired by telecommunication equipment and tools to send and receive messages and orders from and to the command center.

Theoretically, we could've remained in the tunnel for days or even weeks without needing to surface. We were well-prepared and stocked. We had enough canned food, oxygen jars if needed, and cooking gas. We even had a bathroom and a small place to shower up.

But the heat and humidity were unbearable, made worse because we were fasting for Ramadan and, thus, couldn't drink water or any other liquids during the day. We would fight them on an empty belly, anyhow. Our bellies have been empty either way due to the sieges imposed by the occupation.

Our bodies could crash under these extreme

circumstances. However, we had no choice. We must defend our people from such an invasion. Many died while building this underground city, and many sacrificed their lives to create this front line of defense to protect the people from any Israeli incursion or assault against Gaza strip. The brothers' efforts should always be remembered, and their sacrifices will not be wasted. We must fight back.

Sofyan, my brother-in-arms, told me that headquarters just informed him that the Israeli Army targeted Al Shifa hospital and Shati refugee camp earlier today.

This was frustrating. No nation would accept to be treated the way the Israeli government treated us. They bomb our people, control the amount of water we have access to, the currency we use, and they prevent us from traveling abroad. The Israelis register our birth certificates in their records and decide who can receive Palestinian citizenship and who won't. They prevent us from fishing in our sea or farming in our fields.

We are chained by the neck. We have the right to stand up for our rights, no matter what the consequences are. We have nothing to lose. It's better to live with dignity than being treated as a slave.

These thoughts and more ran in circles in my head while my brothers and I anxiously wait for new orders and information. I had my back against the wet wall in the tunnel, and I stood my *AK-47* rifle beside my left hand while holding my rosary in my right, humming verses from the Quran to myself.

"Brother Mahmoud, don't be selfish. Please read the Quran to us in your sweet voice," one of my brothers said to me.

"Sure," I smiled, before turning to an excerpt I thought might be helpful to us all.

"[They are] those who have been evicted from their homes without right—only because they say, 'Our Lord is Allah.' And were it not that Allah checks the people, some by means of others, there would have been demolished monasteries, churches, synagogues, and mosques in which the name of Allah is much mentioned. And Allah will surely support those who support Him. Indeed, Allah is Powerful and Exalted in Might."

"May Allah bless you," one of the brothers said.

"Please, keep reciting."

"And they are those who, if we give them authority in the land, establish prayer and give zakah and enjoin what is right and forbid what is wrong. And to Allah belongs the outcome of [all] matters.

"And if they deny you, O Muhammad—so, before them, did the people of Noah and 'Aad and Thamud deny their prophets."

My words echoed down the walls of the tunnel, punctuating each sentence. When I reached the end of the verse, echoes trailed off, and I suddenly felt alone. But when I raised my eyes, I saw that my brothers were sitting around me, devoted and surrendered as if they could see an angel.

"Mahmoud, my brother, your voice is a blessing for us."

"Thanks, Sofyan," I said. Then, I suggested, "Let's eat before the sunrise. Otherwise, we will be fasting on an empty stomach."

Our meal consisted of canned tuna, mashed beans, and a sesame seed dessert called *Haleiwa* to give us energy and keep us awake during our military duties. We also drank a lot of water to hydrate our bodies as much as possible for the extraordinary things to come.

We knew without a doubt that we would feel thirsty once the fight began. However, drinking water during fasting hours was out of the question for us. In case we died, it would be an honour to meet Allah fasting and fighting. I am pretty sure Allah would be on our side since we are defending our people in His name.

The tunnel shook and sand streamed down from the cemented arches that supported the foundation. It seemed that a shell had fallen somewhere nearby.

I acted like I was as steady as a rock, knowing from experience that the explosion was still safely far from our location. However, the brothers stood for a second, worried. I looked at them and ordered them to sit back down, and they did so, but they did it silently and with wide eyes full of panic. I understood fear might find its way to their hearts just like it found its way into mine, but I had to show bravery for them—to set an example.

I was asked, "How did it feel to be on the frontline in the war of 2012?"

Seriously, but with motivation in my tone, I said, "Hard circumstances like these shelves the hearts of the bravest men. During training, we might have a laugh or a joke from time to time, but it became serious on the battlefield." I added, "The adrenaline level rises. Your heart beats in a way that feels like others can hear it. Your ears will start to develop the ability to listen to every movement, while your eyes will be as sharp as the eyes of a hawk. However, if you don't manage to control your fear before it controls you, you will feel helpless and will surrender to your bad thoughts."

Sofyan asked, "And how did you get over this fear?"

This time, I said confidently, "First, I believe that Allah will give me strength. Also, I believed in my skills, training, and mainly the cause we were fighting for. In the 2012 war, during the eight days, we managed to impose our conditions on the Israeli government."

"Do you think we have a chance, then?"

"This time, my brothers, we are more prepared than any other day to confront them. We learned from our previous wars against them. We have built a full city of tunnels under Gaza. The strip underground looks more like Swiss cheese, so we can show up like ghosts from anywhere at any time to ambush them. We move in shades, and that makes us their worst nightmare."

One of the brothers spoke up, sounding afraid, "What if they tried new weapons and tactics?"

I tried to inspire them as I said, "Can't you see, brothers? We are standing up against them on the ground, underground, from the sea, and in the sky. For years, they tried to lock us up and starve us to death, yet we always found a way to overcome the blockades they imposed on us. No matter how much they try to control us, until we gain our rights and normally live just like the rest of the world, we will always find a way."

I sensed the brothers' spirits had charged from my speech, and I pried with Sofyan and the other two.

By the time we finished our meal, we received a call from headquarters, "*Eagle One, Eagle One, do you copy?*"

I picked up the radio. "Eagle One here."

"*Yes, Eagle One. A new unit is coming toward you within the next twenty to thirty minutes with mortars. Your orders are to leave the area immediately once they arrive to point B2 at Shuja'iyya. Once you're finished, respond to the command center."*

"Copy. Over and out."

We started to pack up our stuff, setting the place up for the next unit and their heavy equipment. We kept half of our ammo and most of our water in the tunnel in case they needed it, since it was going to be hard to back them up if things escalated since they would be at the frontline.

Within twenty minutes, we heard footsteps. As a precaution, we raised our arms, even though we were expecting a mortar group. When the leader of the group took off his mask and I saw that it was Tareq, a good friend of mine, we lowered our weapons.

Tareq ordered his five men to prepare the mortars and the shells then asked me for a quick word in private. He said, "A significant operation is taking place today in the southern part of Gaza strip."

"What happened?" I asked.

"Thirteen of our brothers managed to infiltrate Israel via an underground tunnel from Gaza," said Tareq. "The special unit staged an infiltration into the Sufa area in the early hours of the morning."

"Any casualties on our end?"

"No," Tareq replied with a sigh of relief. "Thank God the whole unit returned safely after destroying the radar system over there."

"That is good news," I said. "I hope we can make a similar achievement here."

"That is why I was sent to you," said Tareq. "We are expecting an invasion tonight. The headquarters needs as many units to gather in Shuja'iyya as soon as possible."

"This is going to be big," I said with a whistle. "Are you going to be on your own with your men?"

"Me and my men will move forward and will distract the troops at this location from moving closer by launching mortars and give more time to other units to gather in Shuja'iyya."

I nodded my head and understood that there were no expectations that he, or his team, would return from their mission alive.

I informed him of the latest developments around the location and gave him the coordinates of the area. I showed him where we held our first aid kit and how to use the detonation button for the tunnel as a last resort.

He looked around and asked me to take three out of his five men back with me to reduce the casualties as much as possible. I checked with him to make sure the headquarter commanders were aware of his decision, and he told me that they allowed him to evaluate the situation with me and proceed with the most suitable arrangement. Of course, we couldn't use the radio to contact our commanders because it would risk other brothers overhearing our discussions and it might break their spirits. So, between the two of us, we had to decide who was going to stay with him and who was going to leave with me. In other words, who would live and who would die fighting tonight.

We knew it was a hard call. However, we agreed that the ablest facing combat would leave with me. All fighters put their masks on, saluted each other, and moved in two different directions, knowing that we won't meet again. It was hard not to say goodbye to Tareq, but I didn't want our men to feel down.

We headed to the eastern side of Shuja'iyya, where my home was. I knew that area very well. I could fight there with a blindfold on; however, I was worried about my family.

I asked my men to hurry, knowing that the mortars were going to start launching toward the Israeli troops at any moment and there was a chance that the Israeli army would respond. Within a couple of minutes, the tunnel started to shake several times while we were moving, and I knew that Tareq was proceeding with his military operation according to plan.

May Allah be with you, my brother, I thought to myself. "Keep behind me, boys," I said to my group. I led them through a maze I knew like the back of my hand—after all, I dug it with my own hands. After thirty minutes, we reached our new spot in Shuja'iyya.

I grabbed the radio attached to the wall and spoke into it, *"Seven brothers moved from the front line to beneath Shuja'iyya. As for the mortar group, which contained three fighters, they head to the eye of the tunnel at the front line, and we believe that they have completed their mission."*

Head command responded *"Roger, Eagle One. Mortar group responded twenty minutes ago. We will inform you about the latest developments. God bless."*

One of the three who returned with me growled, "Why didn't you leave us with them to fight? We were supposed to be with them! We aren't cowards!"

"We don't leave our men behind," I said sternly. "We prefer it if all of you remain alive for another day to fight. Our ultimate goal is to capture one Israeli soldier. If we manage to capture only one Israeli soldier, it will lead to a prisoner swap where thousands of Palestinian prisoners will be released."

No one could predict what the next couple of days would bring to us, so we all eased up and took our rest.

Chapter 6 (Sami)

I have an average, local education, regular income, a mediocre knowledge about life, but there is nothing average about the place I come from.

When I was a child, the smell I noticed most was tear gas, but my only fear from tear gas was that I might drop my ice cream cone while running away.

I always believed that hard work would pay off. I attended school in tents and lit candles when the electricity was out so I could study. But I took it to another level. I taught myself English, asked for books from outside of Gaza despite the blockade, and spent as much time as possible learning about the world from the internet whenever we had electricity.

After changing so many careers, I'm happy that I work in a nonprofit that provides supplies to the medical sector. I want to prove to the world that refugees can give help and support, and not only take.

Six months ago, I became engaged to Noor. We were

planning our wedding, but now we have to postpone it until the conflict reaches an end. Her dowry indeed cost me all of my savings from the last ten years, but that was nothing compared to the happiness I'm expecting to have with her as we grow old together.

Chapter 6-1 (Sami)

5:30 PM

July 19th, 2014

Sami's office in the west side of Gaza city

I read a report Tony sent while shells exploded from time to time outside. After eleven days of the war, I had gotten used to the explosions on the borders.

In the last couple of days, some delegates came to provide support to the organization's sub-delegation and took over for foreign aid workers who were here since the beginning of the events.

Once a new delegate would arrive, I would sit with them, brief them of our latest activities and updates, and answer their questions. Most of them were professionals who had studied in well-known universities. They came with many helpful expertise, like firsthand knowledge of the circumstances, know-how to make quick decisions when needed, and previous experience in other humanitarian jobs. Some hadn't seen their families for a long time, while others had been so carried away with work that they never had any families to worry about.

One of them told me, "I never had children, but every child in need is my child." Statements like these charge me with energy to keep going.

I liked my coworkers. I respected them and understood that we were all humanitarians working under the same organization. Despite our cultural differences and various backgrounds, we chose to work together to make the world a better place to live.

The other day one of the delegates asked about the schedule regarding the donated medical items to the facilities in the southern areas. I provided him with the right documents he needed, but while we were talking, I noticed a bottle of iced water in his hand. The bottle seemed to be so cold and refreshing that the dew from the bottle dropped to the ground when he raised it to have a sip.

I was fasting at the time and, therefore, I couldn't drink water during the long summer day despite work and war. But, at that moment, my mind thought of nothing else but that bottle. I kept looking at the clear water inside and imagined how good it would taste.

I swallowed my dry throat and focused on the meeting.

The minute the delegate left, Yahya started laughing at me. "I wish you could've seen yourself! You were slobbering over that bottle."

"I guess so."

"How was your visit to Shifa hospital today?" Yahya asked.

"We delivered the requested equipment today, but it was tough, my friend," I answered. "The capacity of the hospital can't hold any more. Surgeons haven't slept for days. Resources and supplies are close to nothing despite everything they're doing to save people's lives. I don't know how they do it. I respect all doctors and surgeons working in similar circumstances.

"I met today with two outstanding people who voluntarily came to Gaza from abroad, working day and night to save others with nothing in return."

"That is so brave of them," Yahya said.

"Indeed. It was what makes me respect these volunteers. They are highly skilled. They can work anywhere they want and could've easily asked for a lot of money and benefits, yet, they stayed beside the most needed and didn't care for money. They are only doing this to meet their duty to humanity."

Yahya said hurriedly, "It's so rare to meet such people with similar motivation like this. As for me, mate, I have to try finding some fuel and water for my home before it becomes dark. Take care, my friend. I will see you tomorrow."

Finding necessities such as fuel, cooking gas, or even water had become a daily struggle for our families. We stood in long lines to receive half-filled jars of cooking gas or one bag of bread. We went around half of the city to find one gallon of water, and there was no electricity these days at all.

Life was hard not having any water to drink, or not taking a shower, washing dishes or doing the laundry. Having no water is extremely challenging, especially in the summer. All these thoughts came to my mind just one hour before *Iftar*.

I decided to check on Tony before he left at sunset. The poor man was extremely busy, papers and documents covered his desk, and his phone didn't seem to stop ringing. The bottoms of his eyes were blackened and, even though he wasn't fasting, he had surely lost twenty pounds from stress.

I looked at his ashtray, full of cigarette butts, and I thought there was no way someone could smoke as much with lungs still functioning. "Tony, it's one hour before the curfew. You have to go home and get some rest. You look like a dead man."

He took out another cigarette from his pack. "And you look fine yourself," said Tony. "I don't know how you can function like this, day after day, without any rest and while fasting." But he did what I suggested. He packed up a few pieces of work before leaving his office and told me to keep in touch if there were any critical escalations.

After he left, I made a quick call to my father to check up on him. "How are you, Dad?

"Hi, Sami. We are fine, my son. We went to your aunt's place on Naser street since we didn't manage to find any fuel for the generators. There is still no water."

"Okay. I hope that would be for the best *insha'Allah* (God-willing). How is everybody else?"

"They are fine. Just try to get some sleep. You haven't had a good rest for a while. It's not good for your health."

"Sure, Father. I will try to rest a little bit after *Iftar*."

I went to the kitchen at the organization and warmed up the *shawarma* wrap I bought from one of the restaurants near Al Shifa Hospital. To have the wrap, I had to stand in line with doctors, nurses, journalists, and taxi drivers. Everyone in the lines was there for a quick bite, and then they had to return to their work again to help those who were in need.

I put out three dates and a cup of yogurt and waited for the *Maghrib* prayers, thought about how things reached this point, and hoped and prayed to Allah that things would stop soon. I finished my meal, cleaned the dishes, and called my Noor.

"Hey, sweetheart," she answered.

"Hey, I just finished eating," I said. It was always a relief to hear her voice after a long day of not knowing how she was doing. "What is the situation there?"

"Well, it's less tense than last night," she replied. "Some people are leaving the area, but the majority are still here."

"My parents left today due to the lack of water. I have a feeling it's better to move before the sun sets."

"I mentioned that to my father," Noor said. "He said that he doesn't want to bother our relatives in other places in Gaza and that going to a UN school for shelter is out of the question."

"I don't know, darling. By tomorrow we must find a way to convince your father to move away from that area. I don't feel comfortable for you guys to stay there."

"Great!" she said, I could tell she was smiling on the other end of the line. "That will be a good reason for you to come over so I can see you! I haven't seen you since you invited your boss ten days ago. I missed you, sweetheart."

"I missed you too, my love," I said to her softly. "You be good, and take care of yourself and your family."

"I will."

I hung up the phone, finished my prayers, and started to watch the news while I worked. The Palestinians launched rockets into the Israeli side, but the Israeli army didn't respond. I tried to convince myself that maybe the Israelis were backing out.

I sat on the desk, cycled through the news channels, but within a few minutes, my eyes seemed to shut, drifting me to a much-needed nap.

Chapter 6-2 (Sami)

Suddenly, I woke up from my sleep amid sounds of loud and rapid explosions. Not one, or two, but hundreds! I never thought I'd have had to live through something like that. The earth shook beneath my feet, the walls moved, and a small frame that held a photo fell to the ground and the glass shattered to pieces.

I looked through the windows and saw tons of light bombs, each one of them burst in the dark skies, yet the lives of those below remained pitch-black.

Each of the light bombs scrolled from the sky above down to earth to provide a better visual for the Israeli soldiers standing far away from them. It was a different feeling for the other two million Palestinians who lived beneath those devilish lights. They brought fear, horror, and anxiety to us.

The only pure light illuminated from the moon—powerless and disturbed, hanging in the corner of the sky, forced to witness a massacre to happen that night.

Suddenly, the sounds of fighter jets hovering low in

the skies came to my ears. They terrified every living soul in the city of Gaza. The Israeli army wanted to send a clear message: the skies were theirs, and there was no one up there to help us tonight. If the skies were full of horror, then there was no mercy to take place on earth.

A slight moment of silence found its way through the thick, humid air of fear; it was relieving, for a second. Unfortunately, it didn't last for long, though, as those few moments were nothing but the start of the longest night of my life.

All of a sudden, blasts, explosions, and thousands of artillery shells and air raids were heard. From each metal capsule burst gunpowder, fire, and a hundred-year-old grudge. It was raining in the middle of July, only instead of raindrops, it was shells tumbling to the earth. The smoke from the explosions immediately obscured the light of the lonely, hopeless moon, preventing the only witness of the night from watching over what was happening. If the moon would speak, she would have said, "I am scared; no, I am terrified by what I witness."

I turned on the TV to watch the news. In the beginning, the information was chaotic and it confused me.

The news channel didn't report exactly where the explosions were taking place. I turned on the radio, thinking that maybe I might find more useful information about what was happening.

A man called the radio station, screamed and sought help from anyone who could help him to get out of Shuja'iyya. It was clear from his voice that he was scared, and I heard children crying in the background of the call. There was a sound of a blast coming from the radio.

"Please send anybody to rescue us," the man pleaded again. "The United Nations, the ambulance, the Red Crescent, the Red Cross, the civil defence—please send anyone to get us out of here!"

I flipped to other local stations, and they were all broadcasting similar appeals and requests by thousands of families. Over and over and over again, the significant number of screams and tears that were happening could tear apart a person's soul. I had no idea how it didn't find a way to the heart of the bloody politicians and make them find a solution to this horror.

Suddenly, I recognized a familiar voice through the

hundreds of voices—one that was our neighbour, the one who lived next to Noor. I didn't hesitate; I called her mobile. The signal wasn't working, so I called her brother's mobile, and her father's—no signal.

I stood up, then I prostrated myself to the ground, my forehead touching the floor. I pinned both of my hands behind my head. "No, no, no, please, God! No, this can't be happening!" Panic doesn't even begin to describe my fear for Noor.

Of course, I cared for everyone in that area. It was where my family and friends used to live after all. But Noor was everything to me. I was so afraid to lose her; I'd rather lose anything else in the world. But I was helpless. There was nothing I could do to help her then.

I started pacing in circles and squares, and prayed and requested for God to end this.

I was listening to one of the local radios owned by Hamas. I heard an interview with the spokesperson of the Red Cross, Nasser Najjar.

"Can't you hear thousands of people in the area screaming, asking for help?" the interviewer asked. "Why don't you go and save them?"

"We are completely aware of the situation, and our efforts are covering all the areas from Beithanoon in the north to Rafah in the south," assured Najjar. "We are doing our best to coordinate for the Red Crescent ambulances to enter and evacuate the injured."

"Why don't you act faster, and why don't you send your ambulances immediately?"

"The International Committee of the Red Cross has no ambulances on the ground. Therefore, we coordinate with the Red Crescent ambulances to pick up civilians and evacuate them. The coordination process takes so much time and effort between both parties of the conflict so that the paramedics and civilians in the ambulances aren't put at risk."

"What are you waiting for? Do you want all of them to die under the brutal act of the Zionists army?"

"Every soul counts, and we are acting from day to night to do our work," said the spokesperson. "We urge both sides to respect the International Humanitarian Law and go to the greatest lengths to avoid involving civilians in a military conflict."

"I don't think you are Palestinian enough. You don't care for your people."

"If you please, it's not the time or the place to make such accusations. Members of my family are living over there with half a million people. I wish we had the resources and the time to do so. I know exactly how it feels. We are trying to reduce the consequences of these unfortunate events and to limit risking the lives of the medical teams."

"Thank you, Nasser. But I don't think you are doing enough."

I had his number, so I tried calling him, and thought maybe he could help. I had only met him once or twice before, and I was sure I was not the only one calling him, but I had no other option. I kept thinking that perhaps he could reach Shuja'iyya and get Noor out. But I didn't ever find out because his phone was busy.

The shelling became faster and somehow louder with each minute that passed. I opened the curtains and looked into the city from the western side of Gaza where all the international non-governmental organizations were based.

All I saw was the eastern side of Gaza burning, becoming a haze of orange flickering into the night.

The longer the night went on, the lighter the city became from all the light bombs and fires that were burning everything. Houses, buildings, families, even the hopes for peace and the spirit of the holy month, fire and grudge engulfed everything. The individual pillars of smoke were so many that they started to mix and created one big cloud of dust. If someone were to listen carefully, it would sound like there were drums in the distance from the explosions, no different from any movie that depicted the fall of Rome. The only difference was that this is the twenty-first century, where humans were supposedly civilized. At that moment, I am hard-pressed to believe it.

At last, the signal connected to one of Noor's brother's phones.

"Sharef! I'm so relieved you answered." I was so relieved to hear him. "What is going on there? How is Noor?"

But Sharef wasn't jovial; he was yelling, "I can't hear you! Speak louder!"

"Are you okay?" I repeated, and swallowed my concern. "What is happening?"

"The house is shaking, Sami. The explosions are all over the place. We are in the basement now with the whole family. Two of my uncles left. Send anyone to get us out of here! The civil defence, the Red Cross, anyone!"

"The news mentioned that they are trying their best to send ambulances. Just stay tight and take cover, Sharef."

"I was thinking of moving with the whole family into other houses that might be safer."

"Don't go anywhere that might be dangerous. Can I talk to Noor?"

But before he responded, the call ends.

I tried calling again, but the signal didn't connect.

I thought of going there myself, maybe taking the organization's vehicle because it had the organization's symbol on the side and trying to evacuate them myself. But if the car got damaged, the organization wouldn't be able to provide medical supplies to the hospitals.

The truth was, I might not even be able to reach them;

it would be insanity for anybody to go there then. It was a suicide act. It was dark, dangerous, and I'm sure that the organization would refuse my request. However, it was still worth a try, so I decided to call Tony.

"Yes, Sami," said Tony when he answered my call. "Good thing you called; due to the recent escalation taking place right now, we have a lot of work to do tomorrow morning. I received a call from the Ministry of Health, and we have to act according to protocol. First thing in the morning you and I—"

"Wait," I interrupted. "Tony, Noor and her family are surrounded in Shuja'iyya. Their lives are in terrible danger. I managed to talk to them for just a minute, and anything might happen any second."

"Oh, I'm sorry to hear that. I don't know what to say, but I hope that they stay safe. I don't know what to do."

"There is something you can do," I said. "But I need your approval first. I thought of taking the vehicle and trying to get them out of there."

Tony took a second before answering, "I feel you and understand what you are going through, but I don't want you to kill yourself. We can't allow our vehicles to be out in such risky circumstances. Let's wait until sunrise and see what we can do."

When I ended the connection, I could do nothing but pray. I prayed like I never had before. It was the longest night of my life. I kept on looking at the clock, waiting for the time to pass by, for the sun to rise, for the sound of the screaming and fear to end.

When dawn came, I expected to hear the call for prayers at the mosque, but for the very first time in my life, I didn't hear it. I heard nothing at all.

June 20th was a date I will never forget, not only because of the horror that took place during the night, but also because it was the last time I ever prayed. I couldn't do it again. Not that I don't believe, but I felt that I was left alone during a time that I needed Allah to be beside me the most.

I was entirely alone with no one around: no colleagues, not my boss, not my family, not even my God. I was alone with the dark, crippling terror that I would lose the light of my life, my Noor.

Chapter 6-3 (Sami)

Despite the summer morning, the sun felt cold. Maybe the sun was surprised by the amount of destruction that happened in one night and couldn't warm those broken hearts and spirits.

The artillery shells kept on falling over Gaza. Each explosion shook both the buildings and our minds with it. I don't think any of us Gazans will ever be able to function normally or ever get over this night.

Sadly, the Jewish people have lived through the two ends of the Holocaust tragedy: seventy years ago they were the victims in Europe, and now they are the perpetrators in the Middle East.

More delegates and other colleagues started to appear in the office; however, I was waiting for Tony since he could approve using the vehicle. He was later than usual, and that made me more nervous.

After some time, Tony arrived, accompanied by a senior lady with a prominent aquiline nose and circular glasses perched on top of it.

Tony ran into me and immediately looked concerned. "Any news?"

"No, nothing at all."

"My heart is with you," he said. "I wish we could do something but we can't. We have to wait 'til a truce is called," Tony said swiftly, ending any chance for discussion about borrowing the vehicle.

My tongue found it so hard to pronounce any words, so I closed my eyes and nodded.

"Sami, this is Celina. She will help you in the next couple of days with the department. I know it's hard for you now, but people's lives depend on us," he said while he was moving his eyes away from mine to not make direct contact.

Deep down, I knew he was right. We must assist and support people—that's our duty—despite our injuries. I tried pulling myself together as much as possible and started to brief Celina about the situation as best I could, despite my mind being preoccupied with dark thoughts.

I excused myself when I saw I had an incoming call from my father.

"Sami, Noor called. She said that she has been trying to call you, but the signal is terrible." I was so relieved to hear that. My father waited for a second and then added, "She also said that she and Ahmed were separated from the rest of the family while trying to run away to a safer spot."

"Thank you, Father," I said. "It is good to hear from you. I hope that they will all come out safely from there. How is the situation in your area?"

"There was an explosion ten minutes ago just at the corner of the street, but none of us was harmed."

"Oh Father, that is terrible! Please take care and be safe." The worst thing about a war taking place in Gaza is that nowhere is safe, and you keep worrying about all your loved ones.

I didn't know how to react about knowing that Noor was alive then, but also, that she had been split from her family, which could mean she was still in danger. I kept trying to think positively.

I also kept trying to call her but was unable to get through all night. But then, her phone finally rang.

"Sami, it was the worst night of my life. I died a

million times out of fear, and the earth cracked beneath our feet."

Hearing her terror, I tried to raise her spirits. "Don't worry, Noor. The daylight is out now, and soon, help is going to be on its way to you."

"I'm afraid to die, Sami. I don't want to die, not here, not like this."

"Don't worry, Noor, remain at the corner of the stairs in the building you are in. It will be safe there."

"I barely can hear you."

"Noor, I will come. I will come, honey. Just stay safe."

"No, don't be crazy. You will be killed. I don't want any harm to ever happen to you."

"But"

She interrupted, "Sami, listen to me. In case I don't make it, I want you to know that you were the best thing that ever happened to me. You were always there for me. Please don't come. I can't ask you to be here, not today, not now. You are so precious to me."

Tears were streaming down my face—I didn't even know when I started crying—but I didn't want to make a sound to foil her courage. "My life has no meaning without you, my love. I'll do everything I can to take you out of there. Now, tell me, where are you staying?"

And then I heard a blast, followed by screams. They were the screams of Noor and Ahmed.

I screamed from the bottom of my heart. "No!"

My chest felt as if it had been shredded into a thousand pieces. The blood in my veins clotted and my eyes felt close to exploding. I tried dialing the number over and over again.

Celina entered the room with her head down without noticing what I was going through and tried to ask me for some documents, but I barely registered her or the request because I didn't care at that point. I crossed her as if she didn't exist, kept on walking through the front door, and hailed a taxi.

"I'm sorry, sir. I can't go to Shuja'iyya. It's hazardous," said the taxi driver.

"I will pay whatever amount you ask for. Please, help

me! My family is over there, and I don't know what to do."

"It's not about money, sir. I understand your need to help your family; however, going over there right now is nothing but a suicide mission. I just can't sacrifice the life of any of the drivers by asking them to go over there."

My phone rang, and I was not surprised to see that it was Tony. "What happened, Sami? Why did you leave?"

"I heard an explosion while I was on the phone with Noor, but the connection cut and I'm worried for her."

Tony responded with concern "Okay Sami, please calm down, my friend. Come back to the office, and we will find a way. I heard some news, but we are not sure of the details yet. The Red Cross is mediating for a humanitarian window so they can evacuate people from Shuja'iyya in two hours; come back, and we will find a way to get in and get them out."

I rushed back to the office with the hope that we could use the vehicle and get there in time and that she was still alive.

I entered the office and saw a cigarette in Tony's hand, and another was still lit in the ashtray.

"Sami, I understand what you are going through. I heard that there might be a ceasefire in the next hour. I hope that we can do something over there."

"Thank you, Tony. It's not easy for me. Those are my people who are dying out there. Thanks for understanding."

Celina said firmly and coldly, "I'm sorry for what is happening to your family however, we have medical transportations to do. If it doesn't reach in time to the beneficiaries, it will be too late. We represent a professional neutral organization and every step we take must be wisely chosen."

I can't believe how those words could come out of her mouth after all the hard work I had done and the stress I was feeling that day. I was living a conflict within a conflict.

"Tony, you have a wife back home. Don't tell me that you wouldn't act the same way if your wife was in Noor's shoes." Then I turned to Celina. "And you, Celina. If these events were happening in your country, you wouldn't be talking about neutrality. However, we are doing our best here. We are trying to do our work, meet our humanitarian duties and take care of our families during this conflict."

Celina says, "Yes, I understand, but I want to ask you a few questions first so I can take over."

I responded angrily, "God, Celina! I briefed you twice Celina, and everything is written in our doctrine. You were supposed to read it before you arrived here."

I left the room knowing that things at the office wouldn't be the same after that conversation, but it was the last thing on my mind. I sat in the corner, leaning my back against the wall when Yahya and Omnia came to me. They asked about what happened with Celina, and I told them.

Yahya was beside me and said in a caring voice. "You have gone through a lot. I don't know if I could handle it if I were you."

He returned to work and, as for me, I kept listening to the news through the radio and waited for the clock to strike at 1:30 p.m. so the ceasefire starts.

Chapter 6-4 (Sami)

Before the ceasefire began, I asked Yahya for his car since I never owned one. He didn't hesitate and gave me the keys and told me to take care.

On my way out of the building, I noticed that Tony was watching me from his office window. I was so mad at Tony. It was not that I blamed him, but I started to blame the whole international committee for everything happening in my life and my country.

I noticed the further I drove east, the more the city was turning into a ghost town. A group of people fled-toward the city center wearing pajamas and holding children in their arms along with what was left of their sanity.

I reached Baghdad Street, and I barely recognized it, even though I passed through it just yesterday.

In Islam, we believe that Hell has eight doors. I never thought that Baghdad Street would be the ninth, but it looked like it as I passed through.

Smoke, fire, rubble, and screams filled the street, and

it felt all the more horrific considering the time of year. It was Ramadan. How could these people be tortured in Ramadan while the majority of them were fasting and praying? As Muslims, we believe that Hell's doors are locked down during Ramadan, but not today; the ninth door of Hell was wide open.

The street was named after the Iraqi capital, and I found a sad irony in the knowledge that eleven years ago, Baghdad City was also burning. Is this name destined to be attached with destruction and war?

The sounds of the explosions were getting louder since I was moving closer to where the battles were taking place. It reached a point that I could hear the bullets whistling through the air.

I reached my destination and I found that multiple ambulances were waiting for the ceasefire to be announced so they could pick up the injured. Nevertheless, some brave ambulance drivers went into the area without hesitating to help those who were in need.

These brave men struggled to stay awake during twenty-four-hour shifts, trying to save people through the crossfire, and dealing with the deaths of their people, and even sometimes their colleagues.

Most of them didn't receive paychecks for months at a time. Many of them were volunteers. They weren't doing this for money or fame. They were doing this for their beliefs in humanitarian work and their big hearts.

I didn't know how they had the strength to do what they were doing, putting themselves at risk for people they didn't know, and helping those who were traumatized, injured and wounded. It was the only job in which you said your last prayer every time you go out for your shift.

The area was also full of journalists preparing themselves to cover the bloodshed in the area. All of them were armed with their cameras, mics, and notes.

At least a hundred international and regional media outlets were covering everything live, including key media personnel from all over the world who covered the tragedy. A tragedy the whole world was witnessing but no one was acting to stop it.

I parked the car beside the Al Zahara school and found a spot to stand beside an ambulance. The skies were full of smoke, and I could already see the destruction from the end of the street. While waiting, I thought of trying to call Noor again. The phone rang, but no one answered.

The weather was turning out to be awfully humid, and the sun was ruthlessly beating down on the thirsty, fasting paramedics and journalists. They had been fasting, hoping that God would forgive their sins and reward them with Paradise in the afterlife. At the same time, those who were fighting and killing people believed that God permitted them to kill in His name, so God would also reward them with Paradise in the afterlife. It seems that whatever you do, you want to believe that you will enter Paradise.

Just a few minutes prevented us from entering into the Shuja'iyya area, according to a paramedic who was standing beside me.

Then he got a better look at me, and asked in surprise, "Why are you here? You don't wear press armor. If you don't have anything to do here, you should just leave."

"My family is here. I want to try to get them out," I said sternly.

"May Allah be with you, then. I asked my family to

leave the area two days ago. My parents and siblings left, my aunts and uncles didn't, and I'm worried about them."

It looked like every person in Gaza had someone to fear for in this area.

"But this isn't a place for you," said the paramedic. "You aren't trained or ready for such kind of rescue. Please, go home before you hurt yourself. We will do our jobs." I knew he was trying to comfort me, but I couldn't back down. I already came all this way.

Firmly, I responded, "Does it require any training to try to protect your family and loved ones? All that you need is a strong resolve to see them again."

My effort fell flat as he wasn't convinced. "I just don't want to see you hurting yourself. At least stay close to us and don't do anything stupid," he finally said.

It was almost 01:00 PM, and the ceasefire was about to start. The sounds of explosions started to become less intense. The paramedic told me not to move until he did.

The first group of survivors appeared. Even the sound of the explosion didn't stop the survivors from running toward us, mostly barefoot with the men in shorts and tops, while the women were in their prayer covers.

The journalists took photos of people fleeing, some with bags of clothes, some with children, but everyone was holding on tight to the last bit of their breaths and the leftovers of their humanity.

Paramedics provided them with water and sweet juice to remain focused, but some of those who fled refused because they didn't want to break their fasting.

My patience reached its limits. I tried to move forward into the area, but the same paramedic who talked to me previously steps in front of me. "Please, wait. I know you want to help your family, but we need the truck to remove the rubble and smooth our way in; otherwise our cars won't be able to enter."

My resolve cracked and I blubbered, "I don't know what to do! She is there! And I'm afraid of losing her."

The paramedic held me to his chest. A compassionate act by a stranger trying to take the negative energy away from me. When I looked up at him, I was grateful and wondered if I would ever see him again.

Someone yelled from behind us that the ceasefire

started and the bulldozers had arrived. We would be able to enter in five minutes.

"See, I told you so. Stay close to us so you can remain as safe as possible," the paramedic said. "It's going to be full of destruction and rubble and maybe unexploded shells." He added, "The Israeli tanks might still be around. As for the roofs, they might be occupied by Palestinian snipers, so don't make any suspicious or sudden movements, and please don't hold anything in your hands. You will get shot if any of the groups believe you are carrying a weapon."

The ceasefire started at 1:30 p.m. and lasted for only two hours, but I kept hearing explosions lazily going off in the background.

Since Noor hadn't mentioned where she was, I thought of searching around where she used to live. I hoped to maybe run into one of the neighbors so they might be able to tell me where she was last seen.

More people started to show up in the streets. The survivors ran on the opposite of my way, exhausted, tired, wrecked, and desperate. Many men held their babies in their arms, and many young men were carrying their elders over their shoulders. It was unfortunate to see no one carrying this nation and seeing it fall into blood and misery.

The bulldozers led the way and started moving the rubble away for the ambulances to enter. People fled Shuja'iyya looking like zombies coming out of destroyed houses and climbing over piles of ruin. They were tired, scared, with dust covering their faces. Many were hallucinating.

The people directed their anger at anyone they saw.

"Why didn't *you* help us?"

"*Where were you?*"

"Don't you see us *dying*?"

They aimed their anger at journalists, international organizations, and even paramedics, an act that I could understand since they just lived a horror, something that will remain scarred in their minds and souls for the rest of their lives.

My senses were reacting differently as if I was using them for the first time to see, smell, hear, and touch everything different from what I ever experienced in my life. Fear expanded my senses.

I saw trees mowed into half at both sides of the streets, electric wires sheared, windows broken, or worse, entire buildings demolished. Most painfully, the streets were full of dead bodies on both sides.

I expected the scent of blood and powder to fill the air, but I didn't expect to smell burning plastic.

We still heard explosions and bullets, but the paramedics were listening for any screams to try to evacuate people who might be trapped. They were knocking on doors, shouting from loudspeakers, jumping on the roofs, breaking windows, and trying to save as many people as possible before the ceasefire is over.

A young father came running to the paramedic beside me and asked him to help his severely injured five-year-old son. The paramedic started to check the child and, for a second, I forgot why I came here as I held the father's shoulders to sympathize with him. He was shaking like a leaf for fear of losing his son.

The boy was pronounced dead, and both he and the young man were whisked away by another rescue crew. Although I couldn't remember the man's face now, I would never forget how he quaked like a leaf in a breeze.

Eventually, despite my fasting, I tasted the meaning of sorrow, grief, and mourning for all that was happening around me. It was bitter. At the time I said to myself, "Forgive me, God, for tasting this during my fasting day."

I hoped that my five senses never went through that again for as long as I lived.

"Anybody, help! Over here, somebody help." I recognized the voice before I saw that it belonged to Salem, Noor's cousin.

I, and a paramedic, ran to him.

I didn't give him a chance to speak. "Are you okay? Where is Noor? Where is your uncle?"

The paramedic held me back and told me to give him a chance to breathe.

Noor's cousin was catching his breath, and his face was full of dirt and sweat. "My uncle, aunt, and Sharef are fine. Noor and Ahmed are, I think, they're still at our home, but it was—it's crumbled. I fear that they are under the rubble."

I ran through the rubble that filled the streets, and ignored the threats of snipers, booby traps, drones, and artillery shells. I ran until I saw Noor's parents and Sharef standing with some relatives and neighbors, desperately trying to move rubble away from the house with their bare hands. Brick by brick, they cast stones and debris aside, frantic and anxious.

The mound of rubble was as big as an Egyptian pyramid, and they were barely making any progress. I tried to find extra help and saw there were only a few bulldozers raising ruins in the whole area. They wouldn't be able to reach our side without clearing a path first. So, I flagged down some civil defense workers instead, and they ran to aid us.

Time was ticking rapidly. There was only one hour left before the ceasefire ended. We had to work fast to get them out before the ceasefire was over and the rescue crews would have to leave.

The civil defense workers dug with their shovels and digging equipment while the rest of us moved the rocks with our hands. Heat and thirst made me tired, but I didn't dare stop. Like a machine, I removed bricks and iron. My hands quickly chafed and bled. I could live with the pain for an hour but I couldn't live with the pain of losing Noor.

"I can see a hand over here. Help to take off the stones," one of the neighbors yelled.

Everyone scrambled to that side of the rubble and started to remove the debris.

One of the civil defense officers reached for the dusty grey hand from below and grabbed their wrist. "There's still a pulse. Let's do this quickly."

We worked together and started to dig in the same spot. I was hoping that it was Noor's hand; part of me felt guilty that she was all that I was thinking of.

We kept digging until we saw Ahmed's face covered in dust. He was half-conscious. His mother couldn't wait until we fully pulled him out to grab his face into her embrace and she began to weep.

One of the neighbors brought some water to clean his face and gave him something to drink. Ahmed had some water, and seemingly, he forgot about his fasting.

Just half an hour remained of the ceasefire, and time was moving very fast. There was not a single second to waste.

We kept digging around him to pull him out, but his left leg was stuck. One of the civil defense workers managed to go below Ahmed to discover his leg was stuck between two slabs of concrete. They got it out, but it was entirely smashed, or what was left of it.

"Ahmed, this is me, Sami. Was Noor with you?" I waited for a response, but he barely knew who was around him. He was so delirious with pain. "Ahmed, please focus for a second with me. Was Noor with you?"

Ahmed nodded and pointed at the same spot we found him.

Essam asked his wife to take Ahmed and leave with the paramedic to the hospital immediately because he lost a lot of blood.

Only ten minutes were left before the ceasefire ended. Someone said we had to move before the artillery started again, but I acted as though I didn't hear him and kept digging. I couldn't leave yet; I couldn't leave her under the rubble believing that she was buried alive.

A civil defense officer told his colleagues to pack

their equipment and leave.

I reached out to one of them and said, "I can't force any of you to stay here. I respect all the work you have done under these circumstances. However, please leave me a shovel because I'm not going anywhere before I find my fiancé."

Essam asked for another, while Sharef hesitated between staying and leaving.

The civil defense officer gave us two shovels and wished us the best. I started to dig again without looking at Sharef, who left with his cousin. He went without saying a single word. There was no one else in sight except the two of us. For a moment, it was quiet, and a single lively breeze passed by. The breeze was the only good thing that happened that day. Essam looked at me with an appreciation for a second, and I realized he was honored that I was so committed to his daughter. There was an apology behind his look for refusing me when I proposed the first time. All of that I got from one single look, a language that shortened a thousand words.

After a couple of hits with my shovel into the ground,

I felt a small movement beneath the sand. I bent over and started to remove the sand from the area with my hands. The rubble and fragments of the broken glass were lacerations against my injured hands. I tore my shirt and tied it around my hands to keep on removing the sand around that spot.

Suddenly, I thought I hit human flesh. I called for Essam, and we began to remove the rubble and sand together. A body started to appear, and my heart sank when I recognized it was Noor. I somehow started to remove the dirt even faster.

The shawl I gave to her as a gift was around her shoulders, and I saw it rise and fall. I was astonished to see she was still breathing. I tried to pull her up, but she was trapped under a part of the wall in a small hole, and we couldn't pull her up between the two of us.

Essam started to push the wall away, and I tried to pull her out. When that didn't work, we tried the other way around. I looked for a piece of wood nearby to use as leverage. I found one nearby—there was no shortage of beams. I lay its bottom under the rock and slammed the pressure of my entire body on the top of the wall. I pushed the wood down as Essam tried to raise the wall. The wood broke, and we fell to the ground.

I was tired, thirsty, frustrated, and exhausted. Meanwhile, Noor was laying in front of me, and I couldn't do more. At that moment I thought of just laying down with her rather than leaving her alone like this.

An explosion boomed not so far off, followed by another, and another. It seemed the ceasefire was over.

Maybe none of us would leave here alive. I started to accept that our destiny was joined. If Noor remained here, I would stay too.

A shadow of a man with a rifle emerged from the street. He aimed his rifle at us in the beginning. I got scared and raised my hands. The masked man didn't say anything till he checked the area for a second. Then he walked toward the wall from behind us. Then he said, "Dad, Sami, it's me, Mahmoud. What's happening here? Why are you still here?"

I was never happier to see Mahmoud. I felt relieved, and I replied, "Noor is below the wall, and we are trying to get her out!"

Mahmoud put his rifle and mask aside and approached to help us.

I put all of my strength into that push. The rock hardly budged at first, but eventually, it moved. Somehow, we managed to pull Noor out from under the rubble.

Mahmoud said with a confident, but tired, voice while gripping his rifle, "Okay, guys. It's time to leave immediately."

I responded while holding Noor, "What about you?"

He answered with the same confident voice, "My work isn't done here yet."

He went to his father, kissed his forehead and hands before he said humbly, "In case I don't see you again, father, forgive me, for any trouble I did and ask my mother for forgiveness too."

Essam was touched and said, "You are forgiven, my son. Take good care of yourself."

"Now, both of you take Noor to the nearest hospital," said Mahmoud. "But don't head to the left on your way out. We built an ambush over there."

I carried Noor in my arms exactly how a groom carried his bride on their wedding night as they crossed the threshold to their new home, hoping to start a new life full of happiness and hope together. I never thought the first time I would hold her that she would be covered in blood and en route to the hospital.

Mahmoud kissed her cheek, and said, "Stay strong sister." Mahmoud put his mask on, and left. But before he was out of view, he looked back at me. "I always believed that you are a good man who would do anything for my sister." And then he disappeared.

Those were the last words he ever said to me.

We were covered in dirt, rubble, and dust, and I ran with my uncle through the destroyed streets, holding Noor. Just before we reached the end of the road, an explosion detonated beside us.

The next thing I knew, I was on the ground. Everything was spinning, and all I saw was smoke. I looked for Noor, who was still beside me where I dropped her. She was barely breathing. I checked myself, and I was fine. As for Essam, a projectile injured his shoulder.

I rose, picked up Noor, and I ran to a crowd where I handed her to a paramedic before returning back for Essam. He stood up, walked toward me, limping and holding his shoulder. I put his arm over my back and walked him to the crowd so that another paramedic could treat him. It wasn't until we started to drive away that I realized how lucky we were. It was the last ambulance that was left in the area. I rested my head on the rear window of the ambulance watching shells dropping over Shuja'iyya, buildings were falling and turning into a big cloud of smoke, fire and darkness as we were driving away.

Chapter 6-5 (Sami)

As fast as the wind, maybe even faster, the ambulance reached Al Shifa Hospital. Noor was laying on the ambulance stretcher, attached to different tubes and wires, blood covering her body, and an oxygen mask over her face. My uncle was sitting on the other bench. The paramedic checked his injuries and bound his wounds before returning to Noor to monitor her blood pressure and heart rate.

The paramedic gave both Essam and me a bottle of water and asked us to drink. At first, I hesitated because I was fasting, but Essam drank it and asked me to do the same. I was so thirsty I gulped down the whole bottle at once.

It was then that I realized the gravity of the situation. I was tired, fatigued, sweaty, and dirty, and the love of my life was dying just a few inches away from me.

I didn't know how horrible the night was for the people who lived in Shuja'iyya, like Noor and her family.

The paramedic tried to stop the bleeding; a few drops

of Noor's blood fell from the bench. Despite the noise of the siren and the explosions on our way to the hospital, the only sound I could hear was the heart rate monitor beeping. It felt like each beep crippled my heart a little more.

The entire drive, I wished that it was a fairy tale, that I was Noor's prince charming who would kiss his sleeping beauty awake. The reality was different; we were in Gaza, there was no fairy tale, and I was not a prince.

The ambulance driver ran through every red light in our way. Although the way from Shuja'iyya to Shifa's main hospital usually only took twenty minutes, it felt like an eternity.

The paramedic saw my hands and asked me what happened. I looked at them, wrapped in the leftovers of my ripped shirt. I had completely forgotten about them until now, and at that same time, I realized I was shirtless and left the Shuja'iyya area looking just like the people who had spent the night there, although I had been in that hell for only two hours.

The paramedic removed the pieces of cloth from my hands. "Do you have any other injuries, or are you having trouble breathing?"

"No, I don't feel any other pain. I am okay," I replied.

The paramedic told me that he was about to clean my wounds and that it might hurt. When he dabbed the acetone antiseptic into my hands, I wanted to scream, but I kept it in because of Noor and Essam. The paramedic rewrapped my hands in fresh bandages and convinced me that I would be fine. I barely registered it; all I could think about was Noor.

At last, we reached the hospital. The ambulance took us to the emergency department, and another paramedic opened the ambulance's back door and took Noor to the ICU. Essam and I started to follow, but we were told that another doctor would see our injuries.

The doctor checked Essam first and then came to me. I wanted to ask about Noor, but I didn't have enough energy to talk. I barely had the energy to keep my eyes open. When my examination was complete, my eyes became so heavy that I drifted off to sleep.

When I opened my eyes from a heavy sleep, it was already evening. I didn't think I would sleep for that long. I looked around and saw a white curtain around my bed surrounding me. To my surprise, my father was sitting at the edge of my bed, resting his forehead on his cane. He was holding a rosary and moving his lips while praying.

"Father? What are you doing here?"

Sounding grateful, my father responded, "Thank God, you are fine, my son! We were worried about you."

"How did you come? What happened to Noor, Essam, and Ahmed?"

"Your uncle Essam is fine. His shoulder and leg were slightly injured, and now he is sleeping in another room. Ahmed has been stabilized, but doctors say that they have to transfer him to the Israeli Hospital for further medical care."

"Father, I'm thirsty," I said suddenly. "Can I have some water?"

"Sure, son." He came to me, opened a sealed bottle of water, and gave it to me.

Wait. I felt my heart sink into my stomach. "What about Noor?"

"She is still in the operating room. Surgeons and doctors are with her. One of them told me that she was injured, but she will be just fine."

He grabbed a small pot from below the bed, poured some chicken soup into a bowl, and then asked me to have some. He told me that my mother prepared it for me and Noor's family.

In the beginning, he helped me eat some, as if I were still his little boy. But as I recovered, I managed to hold the plate and the spoon, and did it myself.

I was taken to another room where my bed was surrounded by curtains that prevented me from seeing what was happening in the ER department, yet it did nothing to stop me from hearing people around us talking and crying.

I noticed the sounds of pain by other patients and families, as too few doctors rushed to help everyone in need. Rather than arriving here as an aid worker to assist, I was there as a patient. Somehow, I felt like a burden at that moment.

"The hospital was overcrowded with the wounded. There were five injured people in every room. The people beside us lost their child, and the father went to bury him while the mother and his aunt remained to stay with the other injured child."

I asked, "Father, how did you know about me?"

He said, "I called your friend Youssef, and he told me that you went to Shuja'iyya, which I don't think it was wise of you, my son. I was scared for you, but then Sharef called and said that you were here, and you were fine."

"Where is Sharef?" I asked.

He told me, "Sharef is finishing some paperwork for Ahmed. They need to transfer him to a hospital in Jerusalem as soon as possible. His situation isn't stable. I understood from Sharef that he might lose his leg. It's his *nasseb* (destiny)."

'*Nasseb*' is a word we use when something goes wrong or if we desire something but we don't get it. We use this word to help us believe that the horrible thing, the wanting of something, was the will of God.

When I heard my father say "*Nasseb*," I was frustrated. How could a child that didn't start his life disabled lose his leg? And my father blamed it on faith? What would be Ahmed's first reaction once he knew he wouldn't be able to walk again? The little kid wouldn't be able to go to school or play soccer like he used to, and for no mistake of his own.

I couldn't bear thinking about it any longer. "What is the latest news?"

"The fighting has become more violent, and now they are destroying every house and moving every soul in the area. I believe by the end of the day, Shuja'iyya will be burned to the ground. It's a new holocaust."

My father sighed. "You know, the only good thing that happened in the two hours of the ceasefire is that half a million people managed to escape to a safer area."

"Nowhere is safe," I said. "Where should the people head to?"

Disappointed and sad, he responded, "The majority went to the United Nations schools, but those are full now. Some are roaming in the streets, not knowing where to go, and some are sleeping at the hospital, in parks, and in the gardens."

This was a lot to handle; fear, exhaustion and anger. All these feelings were mixing in my chest. I couldn't take these feelings, so I decided to leave my bed.

My father asked me to rest a little bit more since my injuries were still fresh.

I responded, "I'm fine. I need to make some space for others who might need the bed more than me."

My father passed me a new shirt and I asked him to direct me to Sharef. On the way, the smell of medicine and chlorine was all over the place. I noticed various bloodstains on the floor; the bloodstains looked like paint with one color red, only different shades of red. The medical staff had been working like a beehive, too busy to bother, thoroughly cleaning the floors—they had lives to save.

The first estimation mentioned by local news was two thousand casualties just last night.

Despite the severe shortage of equipment and supplies, most patients were treated in the Shifa Hospital. The medical team managed to save many lives, but so many others were considered hopeless when they arrived.

On the way to Sharef, I noticed that the hospital felt drafty—and only then I saw that most of the windows were broken; I guessed from the vibrations of the explosions. The curtains were moving in and out of the windows. It seemed that no one cared for them except me.

We reached Sharef at the Imaging X-ray Department, and he was still filling out paperwork for his brother Ahmed. When Sharef saw me, he didn't look into my eyes when we were talking. Hesitantly, Sharef asked, "How do you do? Did the doctors treat your hands well?"

I tried to pretend everything was normal, as if he didn't abandon Noor under a collapsed building. "Yes, I'm fine. Thanks, Sharef. How is Ahmed doing? Is he fine?"

"Doctors said they managed to stop the bleeding. However, they have to send him to Israel, since there is no suitable treatment for his case over here, especially with the significant number of injuries. He won't be able to receive the attention he needs from the medical crew."

"What about his leg?"

"It doesn't look good," said Sharef. "His leg has been smashed. All the nerves, bones, and veins have been damaged. They can't do a lot here, but they might be able to save his leg in Israel."

"Who is going with Ahmed? At which hospital is he going to be treated?"

"I believe he will be transferred to Hadassah Hospital, hopefully, this week," said Sharef. "I asked my mother to go, but she insisted that I should go, because she wanted to take care of my father and Noor."

"I have a good friend and coworker who can assist you and Ahmed while you are there," I said. To prove that they would be well taken care of, I held up my phone and called Noga. I informed her of Ahmed's condition and asked if she could visit and provide them with any support they needed. She didn't hesitate and expressed warmly that she would provide Sharef and Ahmed with all the help they needed. I gave her Sharef's cell number before we got off the phone.

"Where is your mother now?" I asked Sharef.

"She is staying with my father on the second floor," I replied. "They managed to take out the shrapnel from his shoulder. Thank God his injuries were treated and he went to sleep."

"I will go check up on them if you don't mind."

The stairs were crowded with people who didn't have an empty bed to receive their treatment.

On the way, my father told me, "I don't know what happened between you and Sharef, but it seems there is something either of you managed to hide."

"Nothing, Dad. It's just hard times for everyone," I said.

Essam was still sleeping, and my mother-in-law, Nada, was there. She was happy to see me and stood to thank me for being there for her family.

"How is he?" I asked.

"He woke up an hour ago and had some of the soup that your mother made," my mother-in-law said. "Please thank her once you see her. How're your hands?"

"I'm fine," I said. "It's just some scratches, and I will be better. I will excuse you to wait for Noor at the operation room."

She looked me in the eye and placed a hand on my shoulder. "If it wasn't for you, I don't know what would've happened to my family."

I thought she wanted to hug me, but that couldn't happen in public, even if she was my mother-in-law. So, I patted her on the shoulder and left the room.

Many people were standing and waiting, just like me, to hear from someone on the other side of the door. They were waiting for any news about their family members in the operation rooms, hoping for the best. Few lucky ones heard that their relatives or family members would recover soon, while the majority broke down in tears once they received the bad news that their loved ones would live with a disability for the rest of their lives or that they hadn't made it.

I sat in the corner while my father stood, putting his weight on his walking stick.

After a couple of hours, I received a phone call from Yahya. "How are you?" he asked by way of greeting. "Are you okay?"

"Yes, my friend. Thank you," I said. "Noor is in the operating room. Ahmed, her brother, will be sent to Hadassah soon. My uncle is fine."

"I was worried about you for the whole day because you didn't respond."

"Sorry, I fell asleep like a baby," I said. "Thank you for the car. I parked it beside the Al Zahra School. I will bring it in the morning."

"No problem, just come to the office tomorrow. There have been some changes," he said. "As far as the car is concerned, I will take the keys from you and bring it myself. I believe that you had a long day. How is the situation in Shifa?"

I thought about Yahya's question for a second before I responded, "You know, Yahya? It's a different way of seeing things once you come in as a patient rather than an aid worker. The medical crew works non-stop with minimal resources and equipment; they are the real heroes."

"I understand, my friend. Take care, and see you tomorrow."

I rested my head on the wall, and my thoughts turned to all the beautiful memories I had with Noor.

I remembered when I saw her for the first time. She was a little kid, playing with her bicycle in the narrow street. She was twelve years old, wearing a green sports uniform. At that time, we were renting the house that we lived in now. Of course, I didn't have any feelings for her because I didn't yet know her. Somehow, I felt that she was special.

Later, when both of us grew up, I started to notice that she turned into a fine lady. One of the most distinguished things I remember when she crossed beside me was a peachy perfume she used to wear.

After our engagement, we were a unique couple, taking the chance whenever no one was around. When we would find an opportunity, we would slow our steps, look around and then look at each other in the eyes like there was no one in the world but us. I would grab her waist and hug her gently like a delicate flower. Our breaths and heartbeats would unite; our lips aimed to steal a kiss, but then we didn't do anything when someone showed up from behind at the last minute.

Damn, this place was always crowded! Privacy was a privilege, not a guarantee. All we had were stolen moments. But that didn't feel like it was enough at this point.

Now, I regretted all those times that I had the chance to kiss her, but I didn't. I regretted every second I couldn't be closer, knowing in my heart that I might not get another chance.

A doctor finally came out from the operating room.

The people in the hall surrounded him and asked him questions.

Despite sounding tired, he remained polite. I gave him credit for that. "I'm aware of how each one of you is feeling right now. It's not easy to wait to know the condition of your loved ones. I have a cousin who is in the operating room as well. I promise that we do our best with everyone who comes in. I recommend that you try to rest, spend some time with your families, and trust us to do our job. We will inform you about the condition of your loved ones once we are done with our work. Thank you, everybody." In a roundabout way, he dismissed us.

"Let's go, my son," my father said. "You need to rest. I called your cousin, and he is on his way to take us back home. Waiting here won't make any difference now."

On the way to my aunt, I noticed that some fast-food restaurants, bakeries, and pharmacies were still operating and providing food and medicines to those who were in need. The shops were stumbling along with generators since there was no electricity. However, the further we moved away from the hospital, the darker the city became.

There was no traffic at all; the skies were more crowded with planes and drones than the ground was with moving vehicles.

We reached my aunt's house, where my mother bombarded me with hugs and kisses. I told her that I was fine, and returned to her in one piece. She was one of the lucky few. She had nothing to worry about.

She told me that she heated some water in two big pots so I could have a bath, and she sent my cousin to buy me some new underwear earlier in the day.

I thanked my mom and went to the bath, holding the pots and a torch to light the bathroom. I started to pour water on my body, and despite the little amount of light in the place, I managed to see how much dirt was coming off me.

Once I got out, I heard the news on the radio—the same news and the same calls for help and the same spokesmen saying the same thing again. People were asking for help while Hamas media was attacking the Israelis, Fatah, Egypt, and the international aid organizations for not being able to provide shelter for all the people. As I listened, I learned that the Israeli army had increased its attacks, especially in Shuja'iyya. It was like they were waiting for people to leave, to raise the volume of their attacks against that area. Yet the operations had expanded in other places as well; Beithanoon, Khozaa, Khanyounes, and no one was safe. Nowhere was safe.

In the meantime, I spotted one of my young cousins playing with a balloon. I asked if I could play with her, and she agreed. When she handed me the balloon, I saw that she had written her war memories around it. She wrote how she kept seeing nightmares, how she couldn't sleep due to the explosions, how she was not able to play for twenty days with her friends, that my father kept turning between the different channels on the radio, that people were shouting and dying and cursing.

I wanted to pop the balloon. The memories were those of all that we had suffered, but I knew that it wouldn't make a difference. These memories would remain in her mind forever and in mine for sure.

Chapter 6-6 (Sami)

In the morning, I headed to the office and ran into some new faces.

Celina approached me, and it seemed that she hadn't had any sleep at all. "Ah, it's good that you are back. How is your family? We have to sit and discuss some important matters. Since you left yesterday, there have been delays for some shipments, and we need to make some contacts immediately to overcome these delays."

"Sure, I understand," I said. "I just need to see Yahya for a sec, and I will meet you in my office."

"Okay, dear. You will find me in the office, at the end of the lobby."

"But we are working in the same department. Why don't you stay and work in the same office instead of me coming to you all the time?"

"You don't tell me where to work and what to do. When you finish with Yahya, come to my office, and that's it."

I couldn't believe it. She had been here for two days, and she was already making demands and upending how we do things.

I found Yahya and thanked him, giving him the keys of his car. He informed me that his house was hit with a shell last night, but thank God the hit didn't cause any casualties to his family nor any severe damage to the house.

I told him what happened to me, and how Noor and her family were doing. I informed him that I would go later in the day to see her and I would see Tony in a bit. Tony was asked to leave Gaza because he had been working day and night, and they needed to replace him.

I asked about the replacement, and he told me that all he knew was that his name was Alex and he was a very experienced man who had worked on different missions.

I thanked him for the updates. We went to see Celina on the way back to the office. I felt sorry for Tony. He faced a hard position at a hard time. However, he didn't ask about what happened to me or checked how my life was in the last couple of days. It was crazy how much a person's life could change in a day or two. Never mind that it was not easy when you thought you had a good bond with someone and figured out it was nothing special.

On my way to Celina's office, I received a phone call from my father. He told me that one of my cousins was killed in the explosions. My cousin was seventeen years old, a polite young man, good in school; any family would've been lucky to have a kid like him.

I called my uncle at once to pay my condolences and apologize for not being able to attend his funeral due to Noor's situation and the responsibilities I had in the organization. I felt relieved when he said that he understood and accepted my apology.

I sat down with Celina for a couple of hours, and I felt that she was upset with the situation, scared and confused. It was an extraordinary reaction for someone who was supposed to be humanitarian. She barely managed to look through the papers, and she kept on cursing and yelling. I tried to calm her down, but none of my efforts worked. She needed a babysitter rather than a coworker.

Despite her age, she was strangely childish. She refused to hear anything I said, and didn't respond respectfully to my thoughts and ideas. Eventually, I was fed up enough to leave the office and went back to my desk. At least there I could get something done.

After a second, I sat down, and I felt lost. I didn't know who to contact or reach out to. In the end, I found myself calling Noga, hoping she could see through the mess and point me in the right direction.

"Noga, I'm falling apart. I'm going crazy, and no one is supporting me here. I'm losing family members. I don't know if I will ever see Noor again, and my new coworker Celina is acting crazy."

"I get you. I swear you did a great job, but she might be afraid. Try to make her feel that she is in a better environment than what is here."

"A better environment? Noga, there is nothing good happening here. Yesterday was the first time in a week that I took a bath or had a proper sleep. I might lose my fiancé forever, and now you are telling me to babysit Celina? I will try my best, but trust me, two days with her are much more than one hundred days of the war."

"Calm down now. Are Ahmed and Sharef coming

any time soon?" Noga asked.

"I understood from Sami that they might start transferring injured patients starting tomorrow," I said. "Ahmed will be on the first list to leave. Please take good care of them once they arrive."

I went to the office and started working with Omnia and Yahya. I had no idea what I would do if it was not for their support.

Later, I received a phone call from Noor's mother telling me that the doctor wanted to see us with no further explanation. I informed my colleagues what happened, and had a brief meeting with Alex to give him the latest updates on our department and told him that I needed to take a couple of days off.

I reached the Shifa Hospital where I saw Essam, my aunt, and Sharef, all three of them with a gloomy expression on their faces. My aunt was staring everywhere but nowhere, her cheeks were wet with tears. Both of Sharef's hands were on his head. My heartbeat accelerated, and I asked them what the doctor had said.

They looked at each other and Essam spoke only a

few words, "Noor had internal injuries in her brain, and it's only a matter of days before she dies."

My heart almost stopped. My mind refused to accept what I had just heard. I was angry and unwilling to give up. "We can send Noor to Israel or find her the best doctors operating here!"

Essam got up from his chair and walked over to me. He laid his hand over my shoulder and said, "*Nasseb*, Sami."

"Don't say *nasseb*!" I yelled. "She was only twenty-three years old. She was a good daughter, and she was going to be a good wife and loving mother to our sons and daughters, and now you are blaming it on *nasseb*? She was supposed to die peacefully in her bed, many years from now, not when she is at the beginning of her life, not when she was preparing for her wedding."

In other parts of the world, they would open an investigation if someone died by such an accident. I couldn't believe that we had no values, we weren't considered humans, that we could be killed and hurt by anyone, and the world wouldn't care.

I stared angrily at Essam. "It's *you*! If *you had* agreed

to leave your place and if *you* weren't so stubborn that night, she would've been around us by now. *You* are the reason for all of this!"

It was only then I realized the hall was silent.

I felt as if my head was being squeezed. My vision tunneled, and my breathing became heavy as if I was on the top of a mountain.

Essam glared back, holding my stare. "Are you quite finished now? Did you let it all out? Is it about blaming someone? Okay, I'm the one to blame. I'll take the fall. In my lifetime, this is the second house that I lost. I didn't want my family to be displaced as I was during my childhood. You have no idea how humiliated we were living in tents and under other people's roofs for years. I couldn't leave the house that I built brick by brick all of my life. I loved my house as it is one of my children. Are you happy to have a reason? Is *this* what you want to hear, Sami?"

I suddenly felt even more offended, even though that shouldn't be possible. I wanted to apologize, to take it back, but Essam continued before I had a chance to speak.

"As you know, when a man loses his wife, they call

him a widower, and when a boy loses his parent, they call him an orphan. But there is no word for a man who loses his son or daughter. Do you know why? Because no amount of grief or sorrow can hold that pain in one word. No man is supposed to live for the day when he buries his flesh and blood."

Essam turned his back on me and returned to his chair. At that moment, I felt that I was no longer welcomed among them. I slowly moved away and decided to leave, and went to search for Noor's doctor.

It took me a while before I managed to talk to him since he was dealing with many cases, and he told me that the doctors couldn't do anything for her, not here, not in Israel, not anywhere. I asked to see her, and he agreed to let me for a few minutes only.

I put on the sterilized uniform and entered the ICU on the ground floor of the Shifa Hospital. The department was crowded with doctors, nurses, patients in all states, and equipment, and there was my beauty, sleeping peacefully and quietly, attached to so many beeping machines.

My stare snagged on the injuries and wounds

scattering her body, and her head was wrapped with a medical bandage, but her face was perfectly normal. She was as beautiful as she always had been. If I ignored everything, I could just pretend that she was sleeping, and that we were not in a hospital, and I was not subconsciously noting the minutes I had left with her. This wasn't happening.

I moved over and gently held her hand, kissing it frequently.

And then I collapsed. "I'm sorry for every day I wasn't there for you. I'm sorry for making promises of having a better future and a wonderful life. I'm sorry that I promised we would raise our children and see them growing, going to school, see them graduate, and get married. I'm sorry for all of those dreams that will never be achieved." My voice was hitching now as the words and tears were falling free. But if I was stopped now, I would never be able to start up again. "I'm sorry that I didn't keep my promise to take you to Jerusalem to pray in Al Aqsa Mosque, to walk in the old city, and to hold hands on Jaffa Street where we can go to shops and enjoy the festival of lights.

"But I'm sorry the most that I took so much time to come over and save you. I'm sorry for not being able to protect you when you needed me the most." I had lost her.

Maybe our love would grow up to touch the sky if our seeds were planted in any other place than the land of God that is watered with blood and hatred.

All too soon, my time was up. I put Noor's hand gently on the bed and turned away once the doctor asked me to leave, accepting that this would be the last time I would see her breathing.

On my way out of the unit, my aunt was waiting for me. She took hold of my hand. "How was she?"

"She is sleeping like an angel."

"At least you dared to go and see her," she said. "Neither her father nor I managed to do that."

"Please pass on to Essam my apologies for what I said earlier. I just love her so much and felt a little bit shocked when I heard the news."

"No worries, my son. We know how much you loved each other. I knew that when you used to wait for her at the edge of the street and wait for her to share the same taxi."

Despite myself, I smiled at the memory. "So, you

knew about my trick?"

She said, "Yes, I knew all about it. I'm indeed a mother, but before that, I'm a woman. I know how it is to fall in love. I appreciate all the happiness you brought to her, Sami. Since the day she knew you, she grew up to be this wonderful woman who blossomed and became more lively. She had never been happier in her life. Thank you, my son, for everything you have done so far, and I hope that she still has more days to share with you. It's so hard for me to believe that she won't be here anymore." She started to cry over my chest.

I put my hand over her head, which was covered by a *hijab*, and let her cry on my chest. I had the feeling that she remembered Noor's twenty-three years and she was trying to transfer her affections for her to me.

I hugged her. For a second, I felt that I was playing the part of the mother here. After a couple of minutes, she stepped back, knowing that it wasn't suitable to embrace in a public place in Gaza. She looked at me in the eyes and left without a word.

The next day, I went to the office according to Alex's

request and asked for another couple of days off to spend them with my family and Noor. I entered the office and went directly to Celina's desk, but I didn't find her there. I looked to Yahya. "Where is she, Celina?"

"She left Gaza."

"And when is she coming back?"

"No, she left to go to Jerusalem," said Yahya. "She isn't coming back because she can't handle the situation here anymore."

"I hope that she is fine and can react better from Jerusalem than here. If she stayed for another couple of days, for sure, she might have collapsed and lost her ability to focus."

At that moment, Alex came in and asked for me to meet him in his office.

"Celina left this place because she couldn't proceed in Gaza. However, she and Tony made a report about your performance, and it shows that you haven't been cooperative with them and damaged the image and reputation of the organization." He put a document on the desk, the assumed report. "I understand the circumstances, but I don't know you. Therefore, I have to work accordingly to the reports that I have in my hand.

"For the time being, I recommend that you take a couple of days off. It's nothing personal, and I think you did a good job, but the situation is more important than all of us, and people's lives are depending on us."

Not a single word came out of my mouth. I felt tired, sad, and angry. I was not sure that I would ever see Noor again in my life. We were almost homeless now, my people were dying around me, and now I was stabbed in the back because of Tony and Celina.

I was in shock after what I heard and hardly managed to respond, but in the end, I said, "Alex, I need to go now."

Through this war, enemies faced each other to eliminate one another. Unfortunately, in a working environment, if a friend wanted to end the career or job of a friend, it was easier to do it from behind his back. It was worse being betrayed by a disloyal friend than to be killed by an honest enemy.

The office was far away from home, and aside from some people in the streets, it was empty.

I reached my aunt's home, entered my cousin's room, took off my shirt, and without saying one word to anybody I went to the bed that was prepared for me. I lay on the bed and, despite the multiple sounds of explosions and bombing, and the horrible thoughts that filled my head about Noor, I closed my eyes and fell into a deep sleep, praying not to wake up ever again.

Chapter 7 (Noga)

My favorite time of the week was when I would go with my girlfriends to Basma, a small Arab coffee house in Tel Aviv. It was small and full of hanging copper kettles and antique lights. We used to go there after we were done with our yoga session. Maybe I will do that again once this conflict is over.

Growing up in Israel makes me fortunate, but also not, at the same time.

On the one hand, I'm living in a modern country with a very advanced infrastructure where I have many rights—I can express myself and live the lifestyle that I want. On the other hand, I'm living with the guilt that my government prevents Palestinians from having any rights. It's a burden I face and live with every time I introduce myself as an Israeli to others from all around the world. When I mention I'm an Israeli, they give me *that* look, and their mind goes to *occupier, Zionist*. And more often than not, I have to explain my views.

AUTHOR NAME

Politicians are playing their dirty games and we end up as the victims.

Chapter 7-1 (Noga)

August 1st, 2014

At last, a quiet sunny day started without being awakened by the sound of warning sirens that would alert us. Today, we didn't have to go to shelters or take cover from rockets launched from the Gaza strip.

It was the weekend when a seventy-two-hour ceasefire was announced on the 1st of August, for the first time after twenty days of brutal fighting. Many lives had been lost. Unfortunately, the extreme majority of them were civilians on the other side of the fence.

I wondered how strange it was for a small blocked territory like Gaza, which had the ability to launch that many rockets into our country, to have been purchasing and manufacturing some of the most sophisticated and advanced weaponry in the world. If we compared Gaza to Israel, it was like comparing a finger to an entire hand. Our prime minister, Netanyahu, would rather smash the entire hand than fix a finger.

I managed to proceed with all my morning rituals for the first time in twenty days. I brushed my teeth with my electric toothbrush, took a warm shower, did my twenty minutes of stretching, prepared my espresso, lit a vanilla candle, and looked at the view of the Church of the Holy Sepulchre from the small studio where I was staying at Nachalat Shiva. This, of course, wouldn't be perfect if I wasn't hearing the beautiful voice of the Lebanese singer, Fayroz.

My plans for the day were to go to the office for half a day, pass by Hadassah Hospital to check on Ahmed and Sharef for the second time since they arrived, and then later drive to Tel Aviv to stay at my parents' place. I haven't visited them since the war started because of the amount of work I had at the office in Jerusalem.

But it seemed that my day didn't start as smoothly as I expected. When I reached my car in the parking lot under the building, I found that it was covered with eggs.

"Not again," I said to myself before seeing that someone wrote, "Go live in Ramallah, cunt" in pink lipstick on its front window. Great!

I moved around the car. I looked closer at the word 'cunt' and felt so disappointed, mainly with the lipstick color! Who would use an ugly pink for a lipstick? It was so out of fashion.

I called my neighbor Dani and asked him to take care of the car for me. I preferred to take a taxi anyway, otherwise I would be late for work. I walked to the top of the street and tried to hail a cab.

The first two cabs I tried to stop were driven by Israeli drivers, who refused to go to Sheikh Jarrah in East Jerusalem. The third was an Arab who agreed to drive me. On the way from my house, I passed by Mamilla Shopping Center, a street built in a modern western style. The shopping center has a long history with many symbols laying beneath the granite and fashionable shops. It includes an ancient cemetery that contains the remains of figures from the early Islamic period, several Sufi shrines, and Mameluke-era tombs. It is located along the armistice line between the Israeli and Jordanian-held sector of the city, where some of my elder relatives used to tell me, "If a ball bounced from one side of the fence to the other, soldiers from each side would return it to the kids." Additionally, recently a big memorial stone was at the exit of the mall that went to Jaffa Street thanking G.W. Bush for his friendship to Israel.

On the way to work, there were many signs and acts of hatred I tried to ignore. But burned Israeli flags and ripped Palestinian ones, rubber tires on fire in the middle of the streets, Israeli settlers with rifles, and closed Arab shops were difficult to ignore. We drove by a wall of graffiti that read, "Death to Gaza," "Expel Palestinians to the Arab countries," "Israel for Jews," and "Keep on going, Netanyahu."

Both Arabs and Jews claim to be the sons of Abraham and follow his faith and teachings. Both claim that they are doing this to obey his wish for the holy land. I bet he wouldn't be proud of any of us now!

I got out of the cab and saw François at the door of the organization where he welcomed me with a big smile and joked, "Egged again?"

Ironically, I responded, "Don't remind me. And this time, they used a pink lipstick. It was a horrid pink, François. No taste!"

"Okay, Noga. I have to go to a meeting with the

cluster group, but I would like to meet with you after the lunch break. Let's say by 11:00?"

I checked the calendar on my smartphone. "Sure, no problem."

According to the news that I read on the different websites, the seventy-two hours of cease-fire gave the people in Gaza some time to buy some necessities. However, this added an extra load on us in the organization, as we had to hustle so we could enter as many human resources and aids as possible in the next three days.

I went to my office and got to work checking emails, going through the transfer of the shipment, called the coordination and liaison administration for Gaza to organize and double confirm the medical shipments and the name of delegates who were to enter and leave Gaza today. The majority of those delegates were experts in their fields. However, there was one person I met earlier, and I felt sorry for him because he had never been in a conflict area before. I was worried for him since he seemed to have no courage in him.

God, I wished that I could be there, but it was out of

the question for an Israeli to enter Gaza right now, unless he was a soldier in a military operation like my brother.

Just at that moment, I received a very brief email from Alex confirming that he received the shipment yesterday, and it was sent to Rafah medical facilities due to the enormous need after Rafah Main Hospital was severely hit.

The situation in both Israel and Gaza was horrible. However, I was particularly apprehensive about Sami, especially after the news spread out all over the organization that he was suspended from work. I don't know why, and no one gave an answer then. But no mistake in the world could justify that he would be released in this way and during a time of battle while his fiancé, Noor, was in a critical condition.

I called Sami a couple of times in the last two days. He was totally down. His voice was so low; nevertheless, he wouldn't admit it or say anything about what happened to him. He kept all the pain in his chest. Poor guy. I promised him that I would go visit Ahmed and Sharef and bring them some food and clean clothes since their house was destroyed. They didn't have enough time to buy any clothes when I visited them the first time anyway.

Dani entered with two Falafel sandwiches filled with hummus and salad from Abu Al Saeed at the corner of the street, and of course, he didn't forget my sparkling water.

Happily, I said, "You are a lifesaver." With a friendly kiss on the left cheek, I took the sandwiches and started eating.

He smiled, handed me my car keys, and said, "I cleaned the car for you and parked it at the parking lot."

With a smile, I said, "Thank you. That is sweet of you."

"Do you still want to go for a dinner tonight at the National? It's been a while since we hung out together."

"I'm so sorry," I said. "I don't think I can. I have to see Sami's relatives, and I am planning to visit my parents. It's been a while since I saw them. I wish that I could but I promise you I will make it up to you."

Dani wasn't only my neighbor and friend. He was also my ex-fiancé before I discovered who I was, and what I really wanted. He was born an Arab Christian, and my brother didn't like that I was hanging out with him since he wasn't a Jew. Dani is one of a kind, and I can still feel that he cares for me, but he knows I'm not interested in him—or any other man for that matter. I hope that he is over me.

"I see, no problem, dear," Dani said with a grin. "Give my contacts to Sami's relatives. If they need any help while you are in Tel Aviv, I will be happy to help."

"Thank you, that is so nice of you."

Dani asked curiously, "By the way, did you turn off your social media accounts? I couldn't find you on any of them."

"Dani, the amount of hatred and ridiculous propaganda I see, written and published by those who are for the war on Gaza is too much to handle. This forced me to turn off my account. Now go, I have a meeting in an hour, and I have to be ready."

Dani rolled his eyes and said, "Ugh, sure, I'm just the service boy."

"Don't worry, dear, I will bring some of my parent's pastries that you like with me and I will share them with you. Now go!"

At 11:00, I knocked on the door of François's office,

which was full of papers and documents from the previous times we checked all the records related to the shipments and delegates. He approved and signed all the documents that were necessary for our work to proceed. There have been two medical guidelines that needed special clearance from the CLA (Israeli border control). He said he would check those by himself.

After we were done with work, François asked me to sit a little longer to talk about something. After a moment, he asked, "What do you think will happen after the ceasefire? Will the negotiations in Egypt reach a breakthrough?"

"I'm not really optimistic, François," I said with a sigh. "Nothing on the ground shows that this war will end any time soon, and even if it did, not much would change the reality between the two people."

François was bothered by my answer. "Your other coworkers have different opinions. Why are you pessimistic?"

I poured some water and said, "It's me being realistic, François. In this land, we spend so much time and effort in building walls rather than bridges, planting mines instead of trees, and creating death machines, not jobs. It's no wonder we don't have a language in common."

"I see, now I understand your point of view, Noga."

"It's unfortunate, but this is the reality," I said. "Oh, and there's another thing I need to request."

"Sure, please go ahead."

"I won't be able to work this weekend for personal reasons, and I need at least one day off."

"Okay, no problem, you can take one day off."

François added, "Just one last thing to add; I will be going to Gaza tomorrow and will return the day after. I want to see how the operations are running over there. There have been some mistakes that I have to stand over and correct myself."

I left with a feeling that there was something suspicious and fishy happening and that it might be related to Sami. However, I didn't dare to ask to confirm my suspicions.

Chapter 7-2 (Noga)

I took my car to the old city and bought some clothes and necessities for Ahmed and Sharef. I estimated their sizes when I bought a couple of t-shirts and underwear. Also, I bought some candies and snacks. Afterwards, I headed to Hadassah Hospital.

There were many Palestinians from Gaza there to receive medical treatment. The staff had been accepting cases to treat Palestinians and Arabs for many years, earning the hospital a nomination for the Nobel Peace Prize in 2005 in acknowledgment of its equal treatment among all patients, regardless of their ethnic and religious backgrounds in such a complex context. In my opinion, the hospital was one of the few peace bridges that showed we all could live serenely in the same land.

I entered the hospital and walked to the Orthopedics department. While walking down the halls, I saw people from the Gaza strip. Still, I noticed that there were people from Jerusalem from different religions and backgrounds there to comfort and support the injured Gazans with food and company, just like me. Strangely, the mass media keeps scaring us away from the people of Gaza, but despite many years of building such an image in our minds, many of us share our sympathies and compassions with them.

I reached Ahmed's room and knocked at the door. Sharef welcomed me with a small smile, yet his face was full of sadness that he couldn't hide. The hospital room was simple and clean, and there were some plastic bags, which included food at the corner of the place, most probably from other people who wanted to help. What annoyed me then was the TV being turned on the news channel that broadcasted visuals from what was happening in Gaza.

Sharef was so polite that he pulled me a chair beside the bed where Ahmed was sleeping. I noticed a space beneath the blanket where Ahmed's left leg was supposed to be, and I couldn't imagine how devastated he was when he knew he lost his left leg. The last time I came and visited, Ahmed was sleeping, so I didn't have the chance to see him or talk to him.

I started to speak with Ahmed in Arabic with an accent. "Hi, how are you? I hope that you are comfortable here." I did my best not to look at the empty spot where his leg was supposed to be.

I didn't want to give him the impression that he was incomplete just because he lost a part of his body.

Ahmed smiled at me but was too shy to respond. His stare shifted to Sharef as if he wanted to say something to him privately. Sharef understood and came closer to him as Ahmed whispered in Sharef's ear.

Sharef took his time calmly to talk to him, and responded gently "Yes, Ahmed, but she is here to make sure you are fine."

I had the feeling that he asked Sharef whether I was an Israeli and if it was safe to deal with me. Therefore, I stretched my hand out and touched his arm. His first reaction was a shudder as he moved closer to Sharef.

I continued gently in Arabic, "There is nothing to be worried about. I'm a good friend of Sami and Sharef. My name is Noga. I brought some stuff for you, see!"

He looked at Sharef, who nodded. He returned to the way he was laying and talked in a shallow voice while playing with his fingers. Ahmed asked, "Noga as the candy?"

I wasn't sure what he meant, but I went with the flow because I didn't want to miss a chance of having a good bond with him. "Yes, Noga as the candy."

I convinced him to trust me just because of my name, not because I knew Sami. I chuckled and looked through the plastic bags that I brought while talking to him. "See, I brought you all these candies, and they are all yours. However, you must promise me that you will eat only a few of them once you are done with your lunch, and eat your veggies." I raised my pinky and said with childish voice, "Pinky swear?"

He looked confused. "Are you mad at me?"

I widened my eyes and said, "No, of course not. Why should I be?"

Sharef laughed. "In Gaza, it's common among children whenever they raise their pinkies that it means they are angry at someone."

I laughed back and returned my attention to Ahmed. "It seems that we need to work on our communication more!"

Gazans might use the same expressions, techniques, and sometimes the same words we use, but they have different meanings. Sure, they are different from us, but we share the same land, so we have to find a way to communicate better.

I spent about an hour with them, and we all had a good time, especially Ahmed, who mocked my Arabic accent. By the end of my visit, Ahmed made me promise him to visit him again. By the end of my visit, I excused myself to leave since I still had to drive to Tel Aviv. I left the bags and informed Sharef about what was in them, and then he insisted on walking me to the hospital's main gate.

Politely, Sharef said, "Thank you for everything, Noga. It was very nice of you. You didn't have to, though."

Soothingly, I responded, "Don't mention it, it's nothing. Are you comfortable staying here in the hospital? Do you need anything? I know a doctor here who is a good friend of mine."

"No, thank you. It's not bad here," Sharef said. "Ahmed has his private room. Everybody is good to us here. It looks like this hospital is familiar with the people of Gaza.

I heard once that doctors from Gaza used to come and work here."

"I'm happy to hear that," I said before continuing curiously, "What did Ahmed mean when he said 'Noga as the candy'?"

Sharef laughed and said, "It's a caramel sweet well-known in Gaza where almost everybody, whether they are rich or poor, buys it during the feasting time. Children love it a lot; however, it's not the only nice thing that happens in Gaza during the feasting."

Delightfully, I asked, "Tell me about the feasting."

Excitedly, he said, "The feasting starts with prayers in the early morning where the fresh breeze combines with the sunrise. Usually, we proceed with these prayers outdoors rather than in the mosques. Even those who don't pray on regular days come and pray for this custom. On this day, people wear the best of their clothes and look like they are all going to a big wedding. Everybody has a cheerful expression that I can't explain. Even the calling for the prayers is the simplest and softest one of all times of the year since the children are the ones who call for these prayers."

"What does the city look like at that time of the year, Sharef?"

"The streets are full of mobile swings where children in colorful dress and clothes are enjoying their time, and at night, men take their wives and fiancés to restaurants at the beachside."

"Do you visit your family?"

"Sure, we do! We visit our relatives and family members to wish them happy feasting, where we give money to young ladies and children and drink Arabian coffee and eat many Palestinian cookies made of dates and walnuts. And, of course, we eat candies; however, they aren't as sweet as you."

"Come on. That is nice of you, and you made me blush." It was cheesy and didn't really make me blush, but it was a good try for a very polite person and seemed that he had so little experience with women.

"However, this year, no one was going to enjoy any of these rituals or the feasting."

Just then, we reached the hospital entrance, and I sympathetically said, "What is the latest with Noor and your family?"

Sadly, he responded, "Well, nothing has changed when it comes to Noor's situation. Doctors believe that her case is a hopeless one, and she needs a miracle to stay alive. My father's condition is better now. Thank God, his injuries weren't severe. He even managed to go out with my mother today to the spot of our destroyed house to check if they could find anything useful. I don't think they will find anything but ripped clothes, disappointment, and sorrow. If I was in their shoes, I wouldn't go."

"And what about Sami?"

"Well, Noga, despite everything Sami is going through, he proved that he is chivalrous and a noble person. I have no doubt that he is a better person than me. He didn't turn his back on my sister as I did to my flesh and blood." I sensed guilt eating away at him.

I held his shoulder. "Don't beat yourself up. The politicians turned their backs on you. Now you are here with your brother, standing for him and supporting him. If it wasn't for you, he wouldn't be able to handle being here alone."

Painfully, he responded, "Thank you, Noga, for your kind words."

"One last thing I would recommend, Sharef, please try not to open the news in front of Ahmed. This might have a negative impact on him."

Sharef responded with a smile and asked as he was disappointed by the world, "Do you think he will ever forget what happened to him? Just seventy-two hours ago, he was part of the news, and I'm afraid after his treatment, Ahmed will return to the same reality. However, thank you for your advice. Surely, I will not open the news in front of him."

"Thank you," it was my only response for such an answer that shocked me. Sometimes, we don't want to hear reality as it is and instead prefer to live in our own world as long as we aren't part of a tragedy.

We expect from a child who lived and witnessed three wars in less than six years to be a healthy and productive person, to see things the way we see them, and act according to what we think and understand. This would be hard even on adults, not to mention a child who can't stand on his legs again.

I asked Sharef, "Do you think there will ever be peace between our people and yours? Do you think there will be coexistence?"

Sharef responded, "Why do we only speak about coexistence when the Palestinians rise up? How is peace going to take place when the Palestinians in Gaza get bombed, the Palestinians in Jerusalem get evicted, and the Palestinians in the West Bank get shot on every corner?" He added, "I wish that all Israelis were like you. That is when peace can be achieved."

I didn't know what to say. I just responded, "It was great to see you, Sharef. I will come back next week and don't hesitate to call me any time if you need anything. I will come as soon as possible."

I gave him Dani's number in case he needed any help while I was visiting my parents in Tel Aviv.

He raised his hand to shake mine, but I went one step further and hugged him. He was surprised by my behavior, but I felt that he needed that more than anybody else in the world. In the beginning, he didn't hug me back but then he did. I made him feel that he can have a shoulder to cry on if he needed.

Nervously, he said, "Do you know something, Noga? This is the first time I've hugged another woman who isn't my mother."

"Well, there is always a first time, my friend."

"One last thing. What does your name Noga mean in Hebrew?"

I responded gladly. "Brightness and glow, dear."

He smiled and said, "That is the same meaning as my sister's name, Noor."

I never met Noor but I felt that we are connected. It's not the current circumstances. It's how everyone is describing this place. Maybe women like us can bring peace to this holy land, maybe women like us can light the way for everyone. M*aybe we are the daughters of the holy light.*

Chapter 7-3 (Noga)

I started my drive from Jerusalem to Tel Aviv. I checked one of the radio stations to listen to the latest news while driving, and it seemed that although the ceasefire succeeded in calming things down in Gaza strip and the military confrontation was on halt for the time being, the ongoing violence in Jerusalem didn't find an end in its alleys and streets. In Gaza, the Israeli government negotiated indirectly with Hamas leadership. However, the situation in Jerusalem was different because there was no clear identity of the Arab's leadership over there.

The Arabs of Jerusalem might not be as conservative as the Gazans who are ruled by an Islamic movement, but they have their own reasons to start a raid without having a clear leadership to move it. The Israeli politicians always see them as a ticking time bomb that might explode any time. That's why they are always using an iron fist against them. Maybe if the Israeli government treated them as humans with dignity then all of this wouldn't happen.

I crossed the olive mount street where I noticed it was shut down by stones and tires on fire. Certainly, this was done by Palestinian teenagers who kept stoning Israeli forces from the buildings' rooftops. They also ran through the streets while Israeli troops chased them and responded by firing rubber bullets and launching tear gas at them.

These raids forced me to take different turns before reaching the highway. I feared a stray stone or a bullet would damage my car or, worse, hit me.

It took me an hour's drive to reach Tel Aviv, a city that never slept. A very pretty modern city, it's considered Israel's largest metropolitan area.

I see it as the most beautiful city, not because of the modern towers, fancy restaurants, huge parks, well-designed seawalls and the museum of art that I keep on meaning to visit, but because it's where diversity and difference are accepted.

Over here, the majority of people are different from the rest of the state, whether they are creative, modernistic artists, peace activists, left-wingers, members of the LGBT community, Arabs, Israelis, or just atheists and tourists who want to be as far away as possible from the two main things that the country was famous for—religion and conflict.

Unfortunately, the city that seemed to be the only real secular and accepting city in Israel is Tel Aviv, in my opinion. It was the main reason why my parents decided to move from Jerusalem.

I am lucky to have my father on my side in the pro-peace camp. I always looked at my father as an educated and wise figure who accepted other people's thoughts and ideologies. How couldn't he, as he is a professor in philosophy? My dad never spoke as much as he analyzed and observed, but when he did say something, it was always something wise and deep-felt.

There was a forty-year gap between my father and I. I don't remember ever seeing him without his long, white beard since I was a kid. He walked slowly and gently, making sure that he didn't make a sound, wearing one of his many blue shirts that represented purity. I could spend hours listening to his speeches and lectures.

My father's past was so different from where he was now. He was an old first-generation immigrant and a veteran who fought in the 1948 battle. He found himself lost between fighting for a new land he was told belonged to him, and forcing the native people to leave it. He didn't want to lose either his humanity or religion. That's why he decided to spend his time observing, meditating, giving lectures in the university, and teaching philosophy.

My parents lived in Neve Tzedek, a beautifully restored neighborhood in South Tel Aviv, containing pretty but small buildings and cafes full of jasmine and small trees that gave the impression of being in Southern Greece.

I was surprised to see that while driving along the beach to my parent's place, it was full of visitors who were tanning and swimming in their swimsuits as if nothing was happening in the other parts of the country. Tel Aviv was in a world of its own.

Sometimes, I feel that we are involved in a war in a faraway land, as we only hear about it in the news and read about it on the internet. Kind of like the involvement of the U.S. in Iraq or Afghanistan miles and miles away from the mainland, yet it only affected the soldiers who got involved in it and their families.

I parked the car and used the antique style brass Hamasa doorknocker with the Star of David on it to knock on the door and prayed that my father was done with his meditation so we could have some time to speak.

My mother opened the door, kissed me on the cheeks, and gave me a big, warm, welcoming hug. We moved through the house, which was full of pictures of my family members, carpets, and certificates my father received from different universities and think tanks around the world. The house matched my father's taste and personality after leaving the army life—a Greek-designed home painted in white and blue, full of small plants and cacti, with Chopin playing in the background.

Our old corgi waddled over to greet me, and I bent down to him to pet his head. He had always been a lazy dog, barely playing with me for a minute before he returned to his corner to sleep.

My mother and I sat at the balcony on the white wooden chairs and there was a small patterned table surrounded by tiny plants and hanging flowerpots, where she just finished preparing a jug of lemonade with mint and another jug of sangrias, the most refreshing drinks during a hot, humid summer.

My mother was a typical sweet housewife. She never involved herself in any conflict. So, instead of politics, we usually spoke about how much she missed me and what was going around in the community, but this time what was going on was too much to ignore.

Regretfully, she said, "I have no idea why this conflict started in the first place. But the last couple of weeks have been hard on us, living with all these sirens that keep warning us of rocket attacks. I don't know how I could handle all of this if it wasn't for your father." The door opened and she smiled. "Ah, speak of the devil."

He came towards me, opening his hands wide for a big hug, and kissed me on the cheek as a father would to his little child.

We discussed so many things; the recent events, my work, his work at the university, but once I tackled my brother's involvement in the war, a strange silence overshadowed the area for a while. I felt that my father didn't want to discuss it, because he didn't want to interfere with Ariel's decisions and journey, but he was also worried about him. The only thing that broke the silence was the sound of cars driving down the street until my mom said she was going to the kitchen to prepare my favorite dish, *shakshuka* (tomatoes and eggs), with a lot of parsley on the top for dinner and roasted eggplant.

While my dad started preparing the table for dinner, I went into the kitchen to help my mom. She was already cutting vegetables, so I began roasting the eggplant and preparing the *tahini*, a sauce made of sesame.

My mom sounded excited when she said, "I can't believe you are staying with us for three whole days. It's been a while!"

I smiled and replied, "Thanks, Mom, I missed you too. It has been many hectic weeks, a lot of work and responsibilities, so a little time to perform a lot."

"I can imagine, my dear," she said. "How are the two Palestinians from Gaza that you are helping? Is the little one doing good?" She asked, sounding genuinely concerned.

"They are getting comfortable with the place. Ahmed, as I told you before, lost his leg, but his spirit is high for a kid who came out of that awful experience. On the contrary, his older brother, Sharef, is living the guilt of not being able to save his sister."

My mom seemed to tear up.

I stepped toward her and asked, "Mom, are you crying?"

"It's the onions, my dear," she insisted. I knew better than to fall for that.

I looked at her and held her shoulder.

My mom started to cry eagerly. "It breaks my heart what happened to this child, and I'm pretty sure his mother is in a lot of pain for her multiple losses."

I struggled to hold back my tears. "It's going to be okay, Mom, it's going to be okay."

"I'm in a lot of pain. I'm worried for my boy, I don't want him to get hurt, get injured or even worse die, but also I don't want him to be the reason for innocent people to suffer," she said with guilt and sadness.

I held my mom to my chest, trying to comfort her and calm her down.

With a face full of tears and a heart full of regret she

continued, "I never wanted him to join the army, but he was convinced that it is the only way to keep us safe."

"He is a strong man, the war is almost over, and he will be back soon."

My mom stepped back from me, wiped her face, and said, "Your father was very young when he first came to this land and joined the Jewish forces. He was never physically injured, but the memories always haunted him and that lasted in his mind for what he did in Der Yassin in 1948."

"Mother, it's different than what it was."

"It's always the same," mother said. "Your father isolated himself because he couldn't bear the guilt, despite all the good that he did later. I don't want my child to go through the same. I don't want the cycle of guilt and pain to keep on going forever in our family. I want to see happy grandchildren someday."

I couldn't promise my mom that I will have kids of my own because she knows that I don't want to have children, at least for now.

I tried to comfort her anyway. "From day one, Ariel was born a fighter. I'm not sure that Ariel fights for the right cause, but I know that he will do the right thing. You raised us well, Mom, you did."

My mom kissed me on the check and returned to chopping the vegetables. I took the roasted eggplant to the dining table where my dad was adding the final touch; fancy chinaware, silver forks, and spoons.

"How fancy! Is there someone else coming?"

Genuinely, he responded, "Only you, my little girl. I will use it the next time when Ariel is among us."

With concern for my mother, "Dad, please keep a close eye on Mom. She is anxious for Ariel."

My dad picked a fork and wiped it, took a minute to respond before he said, "I feel for your mom, and despite that, I gave my honest opinion that I don't agree with his path. But your brother was convinced that he was doing the right thing. A man who holds his rifle must have a cause to fight for; otherwise he is a missionary, not a soldier."

I got upset by his response. "What cause is he fighting for? We are preventing the Palestinians from basic fundamental human rights, building more walls and checkpoints. What cause is he fighting for, Dad?" Outraged,

I continued, "I don't know how politicians in Israel can sleep at night knowing that twelve million Palestinians are suffering in and out of the Palestinian territories every day for the last seventy years." Then I said something that I would regret later, "Father, you failed to raise Ariel the way you raised me."

My dad put down the fork and started cleaning a glass of wine with the same towel before filling it halfway with some red wine and centering it in the middle of the table.

"What do you see here my daughter? Is it half-empty or half-full?"

"C'mon, Dad," I sighed. "Okay, dad, the glass of wine is half-full."

"I did the same with your brother, and guess what, he didn't respond to me, he just filled it to the top and drank it. You know what that means?"

"What, Dad?" I asked, seeking an explanation for my brother's act.

He sounded serious as he replied, "Ariel is a person who acts more than he talks. He is a devoted Jew who believes that God wants him to defend his people."

"Dad, this can't be right. Out of all the people, you know this isn't the way, but it is."

He responded with a hint of sadness in his voice, "True, I didn't manage to open his eyes the way I did with you. I tried to raise him differently than the way I was raised, but the environment around us, the education system, media, the history of our people, everything led him to make him believe that he is superior to the natives of this land. At this point, he believes that he is preventing more suffering by doing what he's doing now. Ariel must go through this journey to experience and discover this path that will lead to nowhere. Palestinians are simply people and people do not stop asking for their rights till they gain it."

My mom came in holding the *shakshuka*. "Hot and ready."

We paused our discussion and sat at the dining table, digging into the food and wine until the doorbell rang. My mom went to open the door, and after one minute, she returned to us with a dark, terrifying look.

"There are two officers from the army who want to

see all of us."

I swallowed hard, looked at my dad, who seemed equally shocked and paranoid, and the three of us went into the living room. The officers introduced themselves and their ranks, before thanking us for having them. They verified that we were Ariel's first blood relatives—*were*.

I sat in the middle of my parents on our big blue sofa while the officers were sitting in front of us on two different white chairs. Between us was a circular coffee table made of glass.

One of the officers started speaking clearly, cutting through the ringing in my ears, "I'm sorry to inform you that your son, Ariel, was severely injured during his mission while showing bravery, defending our country against terrorist threats." He took a sip of water that my mother had offered, and I gripped my parents' hands with both of my own. "I'm so sorry to report that the medical procedures performed didn't save his life in the end. We will provide you with a full report once his commanding officer delivers more details."

Those few words that I will never forget made my

mom bend over herself, crying and refusing to believe what she had just heard. I held my mom, but it was my father who I was worried for. I looked at him. He took off his eyeglasses. He looked back at me and went into a deep silence.

For the first time, he couldn't analyze his feelings, couldn't find any words, couldn't see it from a broader view. He lost his only son.

For the first time, I saw a different emotion that I've never seen in him before; despair, grief, disappointment. My father fainted and I yelled, "Father!"

Chapter 7-4 (Noga)

May 23rd, 2015

For many years, the day of remembrance known as *Yom Hazikaron* that honors the fallen Israeli soldiers has been just another day that passes without getting in my notice. But ever since my brother was killed in action a few months ago, this day now holds a different meaning for me.

The sirens alarmed out of respect for those who died fighting for the state. Twenty-three thousand three-hundred and twenty is the total number of those who died in different wars and battles Israel has fought since its establishment in 1948.

On a day like this, I felt divided between my beliefs in equal human rights for all on the same land and my Judaic heritage.

My parents left earlier to participate in the ceremony that the state held. They stood up for a minute to pay their respects to those who were killed. If I were there, I would stand to pay my respect to every soul that has been lost;

whether they were Palestinian, Arab, Israeli, I'd stand for every person whose life was taken over this land.

Some of those soldiers who died fighting for the Israeli state didn't speak any Hebrew nor spent a lot of time in Israel, but they were loyal to Zionism and Judaism.

I decided to stay at my parents' place for the week. I would rather be around my parents on a day like that than be alone.

I made some hummus and spinach salad, organized the living room a little and cleaned around the rest of the house a bit. I noticed that there was dust on the shelf over the fireplace, so I began taking off the photo frames. I froze when I grabbed a picture of Ariel.

A tear dropped onto the glass. "You would've made handsome kids and kept Mom from giving me hints to have any." I hugged the frame before returning it to its spot.

It has been almost five months since the war with Gaza ended and the same amount of time since we were informed of Ariel's death. However, it still felt like it was just yesterday. I don't think that will ever change.

I assumed the pain of losing a loved one was the

same for all people around the world. However, it seemed that Gazans accepted death differently. Maybe it was because it surrounded them in everyday life and every direction they looked, or perhaps because every one of them lived the pain of losing at least someone. In a way, it seemed that they healed faster from the pain of losing loved ones. Maybe this was one of the few times a person may envy them and desire to be a Gazan since they know how to deal with pain and sorrow.

Things had changed a little bit at my parents' place since the incident. My mom tried to keep the same rhythm by doing her daily tasks of cleaning, taking Mossi—the corgi—for a walk. She even started to visit the synagogue more, but she didn't have the same spirit or glow that she used to have.

But it was not my mother who I was worried about. It was my father who started to be even quieter and spent more time alone. He said that he was meditating, but for me he was just isolating himself from the rest of the world. He was always a calm person, but he was different now. He was not just quiet, but withdrawn, and it frightened me the most that he and Mom sometimes didn't speak for days.

I had a feeling that being a part of his life there was some type of guilt for not talking Ariel out of his extreme thoughts. My dad hadn't shared anything with us since the incident. He's just kept it all inside, refusing to talk or express what was inside of him. It was so unlike him.

Even Mossi noticed the absence of Ariel. He started to spend some time laying in front of Ariel's room as he was expecting him to return.

I tried to spend more time with my family in Tel Aviv now, so after I finished my work in Jerusalem, I drove to my parents' place. It was becoming so exhausting to spend so much of my time driving between the two cities. I started to look for a new apartment and job in Tel Aviv instead of paying rent for an apartment I barely used. I was happy that Dani and his new girlfriend were helping me during these hard times that I was going through. Dani is a great guy, and he would make any woman happy.

Later in the evening, I received a text from my ex, Anat, requesting to meet me because she had something that belonged to me. I informed her that I was in Tel Aviv, and we agreed to meet the next day at her place because she needed a private and quiet place to talk.

I was a little bit suspicious about what she had to say, but also excited to find out and see her again. I wouldn't admit it to her face, but I missed her.

Chapter 7-5 (Ariel's Recording)

May 24th, 2015

    I dressed-up in black with my hair tied up. I didn't want to give her the wrong impression or raise any expectations, but I was also excited to see her, so I applied a very light velvet lipstick before knocking on her door.

    Anat opened the door, wearing a white shirt and blue jeans—nothing fancy—but she had her usual perfume on, the one that I used to like, most likely she wore it on purpose. She gave me a big hug, kissed me on the cheek, and let me in.

    Her new condo was small, cute, and central. She could walk anywhere in downtown from it. She guided me to the living room where it was decorated with modern art. Everything was grey and white in the apartment except for a black chair that I sold to her after we broke up.

    "Do you want some tea?"

"Sure, that would be nice."

"English breakfast, as usual?"

I kept my tone clipped, "Thank you, that is nice of you."

She made the tea and came back with only one cup and handed it to me. "So, I have something that belongs to you. There was no right time to pass this for you, but I wanted you to feel a little bit better after losing Ariel." Anat cleared her throat before continuing, "As you know, I was the last person who saw Ariel alive. He came to our military medical location since it was the closest to the battlefield at the time."

Anat took a sip of water and continued, "When he arrived at the location, he was in a horrible shape, and he knew he might not make it. I told you his last words that I passed to you and your family. However, there is still something else."

I opened my eyes wide and said, "I'm surprised, but please continue."

Anat seemed a little bit stressed while opening the topic. She crossed her hand and said, "Look, Ariel asked me to record his last words for you, yet there was never a good time to pass the recording to you before now. The country was at war, and then you were busy with your family, work, and trying to move to Tel Aviv from Jerusalem."

I felt suspicious and asked, "Why didn't the army pass it to us with his belongings?"

"It was Ariel's request for me to record it and pass it to you personally. He was afraid that his recording would get censored."

The room turned silent for a few seconds. I was not happy that Anat kept this as a secret from my family and me, but maybe this was the only way for it to happen.

Anat broke the silence by saying, "I can transfer the recording to you, but please promise me you will delete it later."

"Do you mind if I hear it now?"

"Sure, I will be in my room if you need anything."

"No, please," I said. "Stay with me." I held her hand for a second and stared at the mobile phone. I didn't know if I was ready to hear my brother's voice again.

I took a huge breath, closed my eyes, and pushed the play button.

"Are we recording now? Anat, thank you for transferring this message to my sister, Noga. I don't believe that I'm saying this, but you are a person that she liked and cared for, that's why I trust you with this. I would prefer to write Noga a proper letter, but I don't think I have time nor capability to do so. Also Noga always keeps on saying I have horrible handwriting."

"True," I said, my voice hitched somewhere between a laugh and a cry. I put my hand on my mouth to prevent myself from crying. Not sure if they were tears of sadness or joy to hear his voice one more time. I couldn't believe that I was hearing my brother's voice for the last time, hearing the last words he ever said. I noticed that he couldn't complete his sentences and seemed to have a tough time breathing.

Anat paused the recording and apologized. But I gathered myself up again, wiped my tears, and asked her to let it play.

"Mother, I didn't forget you for a minute since I saw you last… you have always been there for me. You provided

me with love and care... you always cleaned my room, helped me do my homework, and covered for me whenever I screwed up... your halomi salad and shakshuka are amazing. I was bragging among the patrol that you are the best cook ever... and make sure that you take good care of Mossi... He is one old lazy dog, but he is a very loyal friend, after all.

"Father... I don't know if I made you proud... I was happy with my path, despite my end. I fought for my people and what I thought is good for them, you might disagree now but you yourself took this path too. All I wanted was to make sure that my people don't go through another holocaust. I was supposed to be more careful. I don't know how this happened, although we were well equipped... looks that there is no escape from such a faith. I'm happy that you never tried to change me despite our differences... Most probably, you will receive some sort of medal on my behalf; despite our differences, I would love for you to add that medal to your achievements on your shelves with your certificates.

"Noga, I might not have a lot of time to say everything I need to tell you... and I might not be able to mention how proud I am for being a soldier and dying as *one, no matter what. This is what my end will look like. However, I know that every soldier has regrets, and for sure, I made mistakes... however, deep down inside, I did something that proves I'm still a human and will make you satisfied with me.*

"I made many mistakes while serving in the West Bank, but what we did in Gaza was unspeakable, especially the operation in Shuja'iyya. I ended the lives of so many innocent people. In the beginning, I wasn't thinking about it and just followed my orders. In fact, if I was even satisfied a little bit, it was because it felt like revenge...but close to the end, it felt different. It was tearing me apart... maybe now, since my life is reaching an end soon, I would fight differently if I had another chance... but there is one incident that I'm sure will make you feel proud of me, and I will take it with me as my one good deed as a soldier to the other life... On the third day of the ground attacks on the 20th of July, we occupied a high building in Shuja'iyya, just after the two hours of the ceasefire was over. I scanned the area from above and kept informing the headquarters about the latest updates.

"I noticed a Qassam fighter leaving a destroyed

building and putting on a mask to cover his face... since he came out of a hole, I assumed that he wasn't alone and a group of fighters would follow shortly. I prepared my rocket launcher to attack him once his group gathered... just before I pulled the trigger, a pigeon blocked my sight for a couple of seconds, and when I could see them again, I noticed an older man coming out of the same hole, which made me suspicious about him. He looked tired, dusty, and exhausted. I aimed to fire, but once again, a pigeon blocked my sight... this might sound crazy, but that pigeon was acting as if it was protecting those people. Just then, the old man looked back. I hesitated for a bit because I noticed a shirtless man in his late 20s holding a young lady in his arms... he was carrying her like a groom carries his bride on their wedding day, but instead of the bride being in a white dress she was covered in blood.

"The headquarters kept asking me to launch at the target. I checked if the pigeon was around so it wouldn't block my sight again... the pigeon was laying on the corner of the rooftop... she was cooing sadly... it was strange that I managed to hear the pigeon's voice, despite everything going on around me. I felt like she was telling me not to do

it.

"There were no witnesses around to see if I launched a rocket at them, and I had full authorization to do so... to act according to God's will. In fact, at that moment I was God... No one there to judge, and even if I was questioned, I was fully protected by the army and had complete immunity by our state to not be accused... I took one last look through my telescopic sight, and just before I launched towards them... I saw that the lady had an angelic face with a strain of blood... I saw your face, Noga. That woman had the same face as you... despite the blood on her face it felt like she had the same light on your face...and despite that I pulled the trigger so many times on Palestinians before, I couldn't do it this time. My finger just prevented me from pulling the trigger."

My brother started coughing hardly, and the noise of the machines around him were beeping higher than before.

Then I heard Anat on the recording saying, *"Don't be so hard on yourself."*

He responded, *"It's fine; I have to tell her what happened.*

"I put down the rocket launcher and picked up the radio where I started informing the headquarters that... there was a lot of smoke in the area, and the sight wasn't clear... I kept on looking at them and noticed that the Qassam fighter started to run in a different path than the rest of them. While the other three ran in a different direction... the Qassam fighter entered a building and after a few minutes, an explosion happened. I knew later that this member fought some of our troops and was captured... as for the others, I saw an ambulance that picked them up after a nearby explosion took place."

There was a long pause in the recording, so long that I started to fear it was over. *"Noga, I haven't only witnessed a lot of fighting, but I was also a part of it...you were never happy with my path... but now I believe that I have something you will be proud to tell about me after all. We always saw things differently, but that doesn't mean that I wasn't thinking of my people... I wanted for my last message to be something that might bring satisfaction and happiness to your heart.*

"Lastly, darling, take care of Mom and Dad, especially our father. He might not accept it in the

beginning; try to be more patient and understanding with him. He is lost between who he was and who he became... I know that I will always be watching the three of you from above..."

The recording kept going for a few more minutes without any words, just the sounds of his breath and the medical equipment beeping in the background.

Both Anat and I remained silent until the recording ended. I wiped a tear that dropped from my eye, but this time it was a mixture of pain, happiness, and satisfaction, and most importantly, pride.

I raised my head and stared at a grey mixed with blue vase on the table. "You never know, Anat, when a voice from the heavens may reach out to you, lighten your path, and fill your heart with joy."

Anat seemed touched. "Are you proud of him?"

"Yes, definitely. He might have harmed people, but it seems that he did the right thing for his family. I'm happy that he did the right thing."

"I know there is nothing in the world as bad as losing a family member; it's a tragedy I have never gone through personally, but I can imagine how unique you are to him. He tried to impress you even in his final minutes."

"Thank you, Anat. That was kind of you." I wiped a tear and said, "Can I ask you to send the recording to my smartphone, please? I swear on my brother's soul, no one will ever hear this recording but me and my parents. I want to keep listening to this recording again and again."

Anat said, "Of course. I will send it to you in a bit. Are you okay, dear?"

"I wasn't expecting that, Anat. He was so different from the Ariel I used to know. He was always tough and stubborn, and he didn't care for what others would think or respect their opinion sometimes."

Anat said with a smile, trying to cheer me up, "Don't tell me, he never approved of our relationship!"

I loosened my hair and relaxed with a big smile. "Thank you for risking your job by recording the last words of a soldier to do this for me. I appreciate it."

Anat smiled. "Don't mention it, darling. My job as a doctor is to be there for people, to reduce their pain and make them feel better. If I couldn't heal them, like Ariel, at least I can try to help him leave with peace."

"Seems that I was harsh on you after all."

We looked at each other for a few seconds, our eyes said so many things—languishment, compassion, asking for forgiveness, and most importantly, love. All these feelings melted together when our lips touched.

Chapter 8 (Marwa)

I have many dresses in black. I see it as more attractive than the colorful ones; that is my opinion. It represents my personality; quiet and calm, someone who doesn't respond to bullshit.

The first thing that people here notice about me is that I don't wear a head cover. I wish that they saw the thoughts in my head before they notice whether my head is covered or not.

I spend most of my time reading. In a place like this, where everyone has an opinion and people keep debating the whole time, reading is essential. I believe in journalism as it connects people. It helped me read about other people in the world, experience their dreams, ambitions, pain, life, and experiences.

I hope that you enjoyed my story and got to know more about Gaza, since it's hard to reach that part of the world. This place is full of kind people who are trying to find a way to get over every problem with hopes, prayers, and concern for each other.

Chapter 8-1 (Marwa)

August 7th, 2015

My daily routine begins by standing in front of my mirror to prepare myself; brush my hair and put simple makeup on my face—nothing fancy. I don't want to grab any attention or hurt the feelings of my interviewees who live in hardship. I was to interview a few people for my journalistic reports in Gaza city today. When I reported in the eastern side of Gaza I wore very little makeup, just enough to keep reminding myself that I was a woman and to not ignore the feminist side of me.

I put on a green shirt with long sleeves and a black shawl over my shoulders. It was the 8th of July, and one of the hottest days in the summer of 2015. Despite not having begun my day yet, I already started to feel warm. Nevertheless, it was the only way I could go out and meet the owners of the destroyed houses and those who lost their loved ones on the first anniversary of the third war on Gaza, and the deadliest one so far. I wished these wars on Gaza would stop happening, but who was I kidding? These military confrontations will keep on happening as there is no political solution for the occupation.

The cab I called for was taking more time than expected. When I looked through the window of my room, I noticed that my mother was sitting in our garden, having her cup of tea while watching my niece play. My mom was a successful psychiatrist; she studied abroad and came here to help and support women going through their daily lives.

She saw me coming down the stairs and said, "Ah, here is my daughter, who will become a famous journalist."

"Thank you, Mom," I said while kissing her on the cheek.

My parents never forced me to do anything against my will. I was one of the women here who didn't wear a *hijab*. However, I respected the religion and traditions that many people followed. But I didn't want to force myself into something I didn't want to do like wearing the hijab.

I sat with my mother for a few minutes and asked, "What are you up to today?"

"Well, today, I will lead a circle of women who need

a safe place to discuss their issues away from their families."

My mom was trying not to mention domestic violence, which had increased due to the frustration that the men were going through.

It's a masculine society, for sure. Even if the couple is highly educated and cultured, the man has to have the final decision over everything.

In a frustrated tone, I asked my mom, "Do you think these women someday will have the same status as the men?"

My mom said in a calm and wise voice, "I have to admit that women here haven't received their full rights yet. They are treated oppositely from different neighboring societies. The majority of men aren't violent or aggressive toward their daughters, sisters, and not all the time with their wives. But keep in mind, none of us are having any rights. Men here are going through a lot; they try their best to provide all the house's needs in a way that matches their financial abilities. But there is so little they can do while living under siege."

I responded, "Maybe if men see women as equal and

capable of working and providing for themselves, the problem will be solved?"

"My dear, none of us men or women have rights here. We are living under occupation."

"Men still have more rights than women," I responded.

"Over here, it was always the man's role to be a provider. Every man here tries to make his house comfortable even if it is built out of mud or roofed by palm tree leaves. Once the man fails in meeting his role as the provider he will feel helpless in doing that, and then he might put it on the wife."

"That's not fair," I said.

My mom told me with an encouraging tone, "I know, dear, but a new era is coming, led by strong and independent women like you. You are setting an example that women can be successful in any field and are as equal as their male counterparts."

"Thank you, Mother, that is nice of you," I stated. "I have to go now. The cab is waiting for me outside."

I entered the cab, and the driver started giving me

excuses for being late. I didn't quite hear what he said, but I smiled back at him and told him it was not a problem, and gave him the address of a place in Shuja'iyya.

The taxi driver picked me up from where my home is, from the Western side of Gaza City, where pretty restaurants, fancy hotels, and international organizations facilities are based and expats are living. It is a fifteen minute drive away from the wiped-out neighborhoods on the Eastern side of the city. There were not many signs that the western side of town was at war a year ago, except for a few damaged buildings here and there. Who knows, maybe this area won't be safe in future confrontations since not a lot of the city is still standing?

Maybe if there was a greater international presence on the Eastern side, people there wouldn't suffer, and their houses wouldn't be demolished on their heads.

It was heartbreaking that even after a year of destruction, Gazans from the Eastern side of the strip were still living in schools, caravans, and with relatives. No one had any plans or clues when they would ever have their homes built again. And even if their homes were to be rebuilt, would there be any guarantee that these houses wouldn't be destroyed again?

Oxfam did one of the most unusual and robust press releases I read recently—the one I'm building my report about. The letter, for once, was holding the Israeli government responsible and warned that "rebuilding the Gaza strip after last summer's war with Israel will take at least a century at the current rate of progress. Only an ending to the blockade of Gaza will ensure that people can rebuild their lives and homes."

The blockade was, and still is, one of the longest in history now. I just wish it won't last for another eight years as it has already.

All these thoughts visited my mind on the way to the Eastern side of Gaza until I noticed we reached the Shuja'iyya neighborhood where I reported stories from many times this year. Unfortunately, other than clearing the rubble of the surrounding road, nothing had changed. It was all the same; the scars of war were still overwhelmingly present, the big rocks that blocked the narrow streets, the holes in the walls, and the loss of hope was all still there.

Every time I reported in Shuja'iyya, I convinced

myself there was some improvement. I looked for repaired windows, a new water barrel on the sidewalk, or someone who managed to find some wood to cover his damaged house roof, but in reality, nothing changed.

It was even the same scene where foreign aid workers visited the area to check on their projects. The project beneficiaries became homeless after they lost property valued at hundreds of thousands of dollars. Now they were receiving a twenty-dollar food basket as compensation for their property lost.

At the neighborhood entrance, I saw two children, a boy and a girl, playing and chasing each other. Both carried heavy green old school bags labeled by some charity and wore the official blue school uniform. I felt sorry for these kids because their bags weren't the only heavy burdens they were carrying on their shoulders. They have to rebuild a ruined and occupied country in the future.

In most parts of the world, children would head to their schools safely, and cross through green parks and paved sidewalks—not here. Every morning, children here left their partially destroyed homes and took their harsh memories with them while crossing by the destruction from both sides for as far as their eyes could see—miles and miles of grey rubble, brown bent iron, and broken furniture.

As the girl with the green schoolbag was walking, she held a part of the wrecked swing hanging where they used to play while the boy pointed at the burned swing under the rubble. These innocent souls, it seemed, had some good memories despite their young age and everything they went through.

It was an irony that the world kept on questioning why peace wasn't growing on this land. Isn't it obvious? Simply because injustice and inequality have been implanted in this land. It was unfair for Palestinian children to dig to look for a swing beneath their destroyed homes, carrying heavy green bags labeled by some charity. In comparison, Israeli children are surrounded by pretty parks, green playgrounds and carry new tablets and smartphones to school.

The taxi driver started to slow down to park at the side of the road. That's when I heard small rocks and stones crunching under the tires of the car.

I had an appointment to meet a family who lost some

of their family members. I was sure of the area, but I was not sure of the building—or, to be more precise, the remains.

I asked a group of men in their thirties who were sitting on white plastic chairs about the address. It was annoying the way they looked at me while giving me directions. They focused on me, a woman without a *hijab*, and I could speak Arabic. For them, it was different and unusual. But I also understood the majority of our young men never left Gaza. They had no idea what women looked like in the outside world.

I assumed they were unemployed and asked them for journalistic reasons if anything had changed in their lives since the war ended.

"We were jobless before, during, and after the war. Nothing changed other than we lost our homes. We just sit under the sun the whole day." It was heartbreaking to see young men doing nothing, lost without any chances. Hopeless.

I felt sorry for them. The young men have been in this situation for so long, and now they lived in unimaginable levels of desperation and frustration. It was tough to be forced not to do anything with your life, especially if you were still young and full of energy.

I thanked them and followed their directions. Once I reached the house where I had to conduct my interview, I tried to knock on the door, but there was no door to knock on. Instead, a bed sheet had replaced it.

"Hello? Raed, are you here?" I yelled and clapped since there was no bell or door to knock on.

A few neighbors peeked out to check if they were the ones who are being called for, but they remained looking even after they knew that they weren't.

At last, two kids showed up from inside the house. I asked them to call any of their parents, and the older kid ran back into the house to call his father, while the other just kept staring at me.

The father, Raed, came out the door, wearing an average white t-shirt centred with Hebrew writings. His wife was standing behind him, barely wearing a prayer cover.

Raed was a construction worker in Israel in the '70s and '80s, but couldn't work in Israel since the second *intifada* started in the year 2000, so he started selling apple candy on the beach during the summertime. We call these candies *anber*.

Raed invited me into his house, but I asked him if we could go around his home first to see how badly it was damaged and check how the house was holding up. He did as I asked, carrying the younger child in his arms. Raed pointed at one of the holes in the wall and mentioned that he and his family were just a few meters away from that explosion when it happened. He was surprised, but relieved, how none of them were harmed in the explosion.

Other children from the neighborhood started to gather around us and moved with us as we were going around the house and talking.

We were interrupted by a young man yelling a few meters away, "You are getting paid for this! You are supposed to pay us for benefiting from our problems."

I felt sorry for their loss. I wished I could do more but I couldn't do anything more than inform the world.

We decided to go back into the house. Raed walked me to the kitchen to show me that the fridge was broken—the water pipes were leaking. The house was more broken than stable.

He took me into the living room, which had a separate door from the rest of the house. I sat on one of the four mattresses in the room, and he crossed his legs on another across from me, with quite a noticeable distance between us. I hardly managed to hear him sometimes, but we have to keep a fair gap between genders in our society.

His wife, who seemed to be in her early thirties, entered the room without wearing a *hijab*, but kept it on her shoulders. She was holding a plastic tray topped by a kettle and transparent glasses. She poured me a cup of tea and served it to me with mint before pouring another two cups, one for her husband and one for herself. She sat beside her husband, where she held the young kid who stared at me with his big brown pretty eyes.

The floor was covered by a simple rug made of bamboo. There was a photo frame of Jerusalem centred on the wall, and a small TV which was turned on a cartoon channel called Toor Al Janah. Ironically, the song playing on the children's show had epical lyrics:

"Once we die as martyrs, we find our way to the

heavens." Somehow the song was meant to comfort the loss of a family member.

I asked Raed to mute the TV so we could start the interview. Also, I didn't want to hear such a song.

I asked, "Raed, it's been a year since the war on Gaza reached an end. It seems that your house was still severely damaged, and no one has compensated you. Can you please tell me how you manage to live with your family in a situation like this?"

Raed responded sarcastically, "Compensated, you said? In the beginning, I was angry and upset because no one supported us and left us almost homeless, but now I see it as God's will. Thank God for everything. I don't think there is enough money in the world to compensate for what happened to us. I was lucky that I haven't lost any of my children or my wife, but not everyone around us was as fortunate as we are." Raed points to the sky every time he mentioned God or Allah. "I spent my whole life trying to build this house. Forty years of hard work disappeared in one night. Even when I tried to fix it myself, I couldn't because no cement or building material is allowed to enter due to the blockade. I was lucky to buy half a bag of cement from the black market to fix the bathroom. I only bought half a bag because I couldn't afford the full bag."

"Did you think of renting another house or living with a relative until your home was fixed?"

"I definitely won't rent because I can't afford it. But also I don't want to leave the area that I was born and raised in even if it is destroyed. I have three children and I consider my house the fourth. True, it's damaged now, but someday it will return to how it was before."

Raed added, "Undoubtedly, any of my relatives would take us in a heartbeat if needed. We as Palestinians are known for our generosity. However, I don't want to be a heavy guest, since they won't have enough space for my whole family. They were kind enough to have us during unfortunate events."

I turned to his wife. "What kind of hurdles do you face in your day-to-day life?"

She looked at her husband as if she was asking for permission to talk. When he nodded for her to respond, she finally answered, "Well, it's tough to keep this house clean. Last winter, it was cold, and the house was full of water because of the rain that kept on pouring. The summer isn't any better since dust, dirt, and insects keep on finding their way into our house. I do my best to keep it clean because this affects my children's health. I don't recall a week passing by since the war without me taking one of them to the clinic." She sighed heavily. "I also find it hard to cook for my family with no proper oven and no refrigerator. Sometimes, while I'm cooking, I see myself living in the stone age if it wasn't for the television whenever the electricity is available."

I directed my last question to Raed. "Who is to blame for the situation you are living in now?"

A sad smile shaped his face. "So many governments, politicians, and parties to blame, yet no one will stand up to take responsibility."

I thanked the family for their hospitality and time. Raed, his wife, and one of the children walked me to the front door. On the door step and before I left, Raed gave me an apple candy. I tried giving him money for it, but he insisted it was a gift and he refused to take any money.

The minute I exited, I heard a kid questioning his mother, "How come she isn't covering her head with a *hijab?*"

I smiled and headed back to the taxi, feeling sorry and sad that my hair was the most unusual thing for a kid who was living in such conditions. While the taxi started to move down the small lanes, I checked my schedule for an opening of an orphanage today in the area.

Just then, I noticed a child almost ten years old, standing on one leg and using two crutches to balance himself, heading toward a group of children. I recognized him immediately as Noor's brother, Ahmed.

I asked the driver to wait so I could get out and approach him. "Hi, Ahmed. How are you, darling? Do you remember me?"

Excited, he said, "Yes, you are Noor's friend. I'm doing well, thanks for asking."

"What are you doing here? Didn't your father move to another area?"

"I came with my father to visit some relatives. Later, we are going to visit Sami and participate in the ceremony of opening a new orphanage."

Ahmed's father, Essam, appeared, and I had a brief

chat with him. I decided to go with them and offered them a ride since we were all heading in the same direction.

The residence, located on one of the corners, included two small buildings painted in white and a tiny garden decorated with balloons. I noticed on the gate of the facility a large sign that read, "Welcome to Noor's Orphanage."

I felt that the sign was so big for the size of the residence. Maybe it was symbolic for Sami.

People gathered to witness the opening of the orphanage. A couple of officials and some heads of families lined-up to congratulate Sami on the opening. He distributed smiles and handshakes with everybody so warmly, but when I entered, he welcomed me by putting his right hand over his chest instead of shaking my hand and winked. I did the same to greet him and winked back, another thing we have to please society with.

I took my place on one of the white plastic chairs at the small garden beside Ahmed and his father, waiting for the ceremony to start.

Ten minutes later, Sami stood, along with two small

kids, the three of them dressed in ironed, clean suits. He was wearing a black suit with golden buttons. I almost missed it, but I realized that it was the suit for the wedding that never took place. Noor once showed me a photo of it after he bought it, and I remembered commenting on the golden buttons to her.

Most of the audience had no clue about the suit; he was honoring Noor in every way possible. He was celebrating a wedding ceremony that never happened.

Sami began his speech:

"In the name of Allah, ladies and gentlemen, *Al Slam Alekom*. It's an honor for the working staff and for me to have you here in the opening of our small organization that I prefer to call Home of Hope, and we decided to name it "Noor". Noor means *light*, and our aim here is to lighten the road of these children who lost their loved ones during the tragic war that took place last year. Nothing in the world can compensate a child for not having a mother to talk to or a father's hug, but we will try our best to create a new family, looking after each one of them to shape a new future for them and our country."

The crowd applauded; once they were done, Sami kept going.

"Some questioned why the institution is located in Shuja'iyya, in the middle of the destruction. I believe that they are the ones who will rebuild the east side of Gaza again, and once they do that, they will preserve it. Thank you for your kindness and time."

The small audience included some local businessmen who funded the orphanage and some small local organizations who provided materials for the place. They went inside for a tour of the building.

In Gaza, no matter how little they have, they always find a way to give and donate when they can.

I stayed in my place until almost everyone left, waiting for the right moment to approach Sami.

With a smile, I reached out to him. "Congratulations, Sami! I hope the place will bring joy and happiness to your heart and the children's hearts as well."

"Thanks, Marwa. I appreciate that you had time to come and join us."

To encourage him, I said, "Of course! I'm happy

when people can achieve their dreams, and you managed to reach yours."

Though Sami was smiling, his voice was sad, "Actually, it was Noor's dream before it was mine. If it weren't for her vision, I wouldn't have the motivation to complete it."

"I know, Sami," I said. "May her soul rest in peace. I miss her a lot."

"You were so special to her. She used to tell me that all her secrets were with you. I'm happy that she had you on her side."

I felt grateful. "We were best friends, as you know. Take care, Sami. Goodbye."

The poor man didn't heal from her absence. I left the ceremony, sat in the back seat of the taxi, and asked the driver to take me back home.

I looked through the window at the clear blue sky, and my head was full of only one subject while I was going back home; my dear friend Noor.

Later I looked at my bag, took out my notebook, and started to make small squares joined to each other, something I liked to draw when I'm thinking, or when I wanted to separate myself from the world.

I looked through the photos that I took during the ceremony; they were beautiful, and everyone was happy and excited about the achievement, especially Sami in his wedding suit. I remember how I went to Noor's place a year ago, and I commented on Sami's suit. She showed me her wedding dress, the bouquet she would throw, and we worked on the vows together. That was the last time I saw Noor.

Suddenly, I said in a high voice, "The vows."

I remembered assisting Noor in her vows on one of my notebooks. I should have given them to Sami a long time ago. I couldn't believe that I never thought about it until just now.

I asked the driver to go faster. I was filled with a desire to find the vows and return to Sami.

Chapter 8-2 (Marwa)

It was my second time in Shuja'iyya today. Being in this place once was enough to remind a person how much humans were capable of destruction. I didn't know how people lived here and found peace while everything reminded them of war.

On the way, I called Sami; his cell was off. I turned my attention to head to the orphanage. The taxi driver stopped in front of the orphanage, and I entered the administration office and asked about Sami. His assistant told me that he just left ten minutes ago. Drat!

I went to his home nearby and asked about him. His sister informed me that he planned to visit the cemetery on the eastern side beside the borders. That's probably why the cell signal wasn't working. So, I relayed the information to the taxi driver, and we headed off.

We reached the graveyard. It was quiet and peaceful.

I put on a scarf that I always kept in my bag and entered the graveyard. I'm not religious, but I respect the dead, and there is a lot in my country; therefore, I read within my heart the usual prayers that Muslims say before entering any graveyard, "*Oh inmates of the graves, Salaam–Peace–on you. Allah forgives us and you all. You left first, and we will be coming later.*"

There was Sami, exactly where I expected to see him, bending on one knee. He was looking at Noor's grave as if she was still alive and he was proposing. I didn't see him saying anything, but the way he looked at the grave said a lot. For us, she left the world, but for him, she never left his heart.

Sami saw me coming from a distance, so he stood and rubbed the dirt off his pants. Then, he offered me a mixed smile of surprise and greeting. "I didn't expect you to be here."

I came to a stop beside him. "You know; I didn't have any doubts that I was going to find you here."

He responded with a genuine smile, "It must be lucky to see you twice in one day. But why are you here? Are you here to pay your respects to Noor, too?"

"Yes, Sami, but there is another reason, too, and it's

perfect that you are here. Honestly, I'm happy and sad at the same time to see you here."

"Hmmm, and is this a mystery or something?"

I took a breath. "Listen, Sami, I'm happy that you are loyal to Noor. You kept on cherishing her, visiting her family, and you even named the orphanage after her. However, darling, don't forget that she left, and it's time for you to move on. I'm not saying to forget her; I'm just asking that you may start a new life, thinking of yourself."

"I wish it was that simple, Marwa, but I'm afraid I will remember her until the day I lay beside her."

I looked in my bag and said, "You know Sami; usually, I don't see someone like you, and this is something I admire. That's why I came to deliver something for you. I was supposed to give it to you a long time ago. So I hope that you see this as closure." I handed him the letter and told him. "This was from Noor; these were her vows."

Chapter 8-3 (Noor's Letter to Sami)

10/07/2014

Sami,

My love, thank you for the great time we had together. A lot of beautiful memories I had with you, and many more to come.

We did a lot together in an open-air prison; we attended cultural events, journalism discussions, held private parties, reported stories in Gaza, exchanged books and thoughts, comforting each other and our friends in hard times.

But for sure my favorite times were when we went to the beach. Do you remember, my love, when we went to the beach and we started running? I knew that you didn't put any effort to make me win. But, by doing that, you won my heart, knowing how much you loved me. So, it's either that, or you are slow.

You made my life in these two years that I knew you pretty, exciting, and colorful. I wish that I knew you way before.

Regardless, you have always been there for me in challenging and good times. You always managed to put a smile on my face. Furthermore, there are no words that can describe you. I'm happy that we can achieve all our dreams together.

I promised that you will always have a precious place in my life, mind, and soul, knowing for sure no one will ever take your place in my heart.

Therefore, I vow that I will take care of you, our future children, and keep loving you forever.

In the end, I promise that I will always be there for you 'till the last day of my life, my *mon Cheri*. ♡

Chapter 8-4 (Marwa)

After Sami read the letter he raised his face to the sky , then looked back at Noor's grave. He tried to hold back his tears, however, a single tear found its way on his cheek. He was silent for a couple of minutes, the only sound that broke the silence was the sound of wind skittering the sand across the ground.

I broke the silence. "She wrote this and she wanted to say this in front of everybody at your wedding. Somehow this is similar to the vows that the westerners do in their marriages; she always thought of doing such a thing to show everyone how much you mean to her."

A small, satisfying smile found its way across Sami's face. I hadn't seen a comforting smile on his face for a while. It was like he needed to hear this news, and in a way, it brought life to his deprived soul again. This news was no different from when it rained over a desert, not enough to turn the desert into a green area, but enough to bring life back to a dry territory.

Sami said, "You know, we once agreed if we ever had a girl, we would name her Elena. You might ask why that name. It's not a common Arab name. It was after Elena. She always thought of herself as a citizen of the world, not to a particular nation. She was eager to learn about other cultures." Sami's sad smile darkened. "I don't know how she had faith in the world. The world dramatically failed her."

He looked at me and continued sadly, "The world failed her, failed me, failed us Palestinians over and over again. They don't know what it means to live under occupation, to pass through checkpoints, to delay your dreams for another day, living in an open-air prison, not being able to leave or complete your studies, all our children know is death and pain."

I moved closer to Sami and held his hand tightly. "If the world failed her, you didn't. Look at you. You managed to build an orphanage and named it after her to keep her memory alive. The orphanage is a symbol of everything she lived and died for. Maybe these children will see better days than what we saw."

I walked closer to her grave and placed my hand on the headstone. "We have to cherish her thoughts and dreams.

We have to believe that there is still good out there. It's on us to spread our voices as far as we can, to make the world hear that we want to live in peace. Like everyone else, we want dignity, and we want our human rights."

Sami said intensely, "You know me very well. For most of my life, I believed in that. I was dreaming for justice to take place in Palestine. I expect our humanity to be valued and our dignity to be respected. I expect not to be labeled as a terrorist because we ask for our rights. I expected not to be threatened by cutting aids and support because we went to the International courts and asked for justice there. But, unfortunately, the world sees us and dehumanize us; no one cares for the occupation and how we are treated. We are treated as slaves, and that isn't acceptable."

Sami yelled with frustration, "I assure you the dead in the graveyard in this desert hear us as much as the world does. I even started to believe that the dead beneath us might be more alive than the world leaders and politicians watching us from their ivory offices."

Sami lifted some sand from the ground in his hand and said in a lower tone, "Noor is so young to be under these sands. I have begun to give up on the free world that watches us standing behind the walls and checkpoints and doesn't see us, not to mention seeing us."

I stepped closer to him and said, "I can't believe that I'm saying this to you; you always believed that bridges must be built, not walls."

Sami replied ironically, "What kind of bridges do you want us to build? We aren't even capable of rebuilding our destroyed homes. Have you seen what happened to Gaza? It's piles and piles of rubble and dead dreams. So which walls do you want us to take, the physical ones surrounding Gaza and the West Bank or the ones that grow in our hearts every time this ugly occupation keeps on humiliating us and treating us with no dignity as we are not humans?"

I raised my voice. "We can take all the wall, and the world will help us do so! The world is full of people who are willing to stand for justice; you yourself are a good example!"

Sami, in a fast, furious beat, said, "Look at Noor's family. Their home was destroyed, Noor passed away, her brother Mahmoud was captured, and now he is in Israeli jails for many years to come. Sharef is trying to leave the country for a year to complete his studies, but the blockade prevents him from doing so. And Ahmed, who lost his leg and will never be whole again."

Sami walked around me; then he sounded defeated when he said, "What do you expect from a society whose youth is either dead, jailed, injured, or just wants to abandon this place?" He sighed. "Living in a place like Gaza might kill your soul and heart. Then, slowly and without permission, frustration and anger slip into you."

I have never seen Sami this upset before. People used to come to Sami since he was a good listener and usually found a way to cheer people. "Then what is the solution?"

He calmed down and said, "At this point, there is none. I don't see any near solution for now. I feel disappointed to repeatedly live the same scenario; we are going in circles. Israel pressures us till we can't take it anymore. We raise up and stand for ourselves. Israel brutally crushes our lives and dreams, and then the world gives us some attention along with aid and bandages till the next round starts again."

I asked, "Then leaving the country is the answer?"

Sami looked at me, and a slight smile tugged at his lips. "If all the educated youth left this country, who would rebuild it? Who would be here for people like Noor's father and mother? Who would be here for the orphans? Who would be here to comfort the victims? It's not easy to accept our loss. I mean, look at me. It's been a year and I still can't get over what happened to Noor."

He stopped for a second and then said, "But we must remain strong because in the future, we have a long path to walk. Freedom will come someday. Till then we have to rebuild the country."

I smiled back at him and comforted him by saying, "I'm happy to see you still see some light for the future."

Sami said, "Let's go, my friend. It's getting late. I believe that Noor is happy that both of us came to visit her today."

On the way to the cab, I asked Sami if he was excited for the orphanage—anything to lighten his mood.

"Yes! These children went through a lot. I will make sure to comfort them and make them happy as much as possible."

"Do you regret quitting your job?"

"Sometimes I miss my job," he replied. "But I wanted to make Noor's dream come alive."

Just then, I received a text message that made me sigh with a smile.

He asked curiously, "What was that about?"

I replied, "A friend is saying farewell because he is leaving the Gaza strip for good."

He inquired again, "Do I know him?"

I tried to make it short. "I'm not sure if you do. His name is Nasser Najjar."

"Nasser Najjar?" Sami said. "That name is familiar. Isn't he the guy from the Red Cross? Is he leaving because of the war?"

"I don't think he left because of war," I said. "He told me once before leaving that two things are devastating—living a war and letting go of a true love."

"Where did he go?"

"Not sure yet, but he has a long journey to take and quite a few stories to tell."

Sami said sarcastically, "Your sigh and what you said about him doesn't sound like he was only a friend."

I smiled back at Sami, knowing for sure that he had caught me. "Let's go, Sami. It's getting late."

The car started moving, and I opened the window, letting the wind play with my hair and wipe away a tear that escaped from my eye, hoping that Sami didn't catch it. The sun was setting, bathing the world in a final warm embrace before the night arrived. *Farewell, Nasser. Until we meet again someday.*

Made in the USA
Columbia, SC
02 November 2024

53aaa5fd-e6c6-4d13-8373-13912e785f2cR01